LOVE AND GRAVITY

REBEL CARTER

VIOLET GAZE PRESS

Cover Illustration by Fatima Ghuloom of Qamber Kids

Cover Layout by Qamber Designs and Media

Edited by Lena Tudor

Published by Violet Gaze Press

20-22 Wenlock Rd

London

www.violetgazepress.com

❀ Created with Vellum

For Brittany and Lena.
You are my heart. You are my never-fail family.
We are making our dreams come true one book at a time.

PROLOGUE

To:G.Munoz@CERN.cl
From:Anton@KOVT.com
2:38 AM (Twenty-two minutes ago)

G. Muñoz,

The faint strains of a melancholic fiddle sound while I stare out my window.

The war is long and hard. I fear we might not make it through the winter on our current provisions, and I find the company tedious. I suffer in quiet indignation and hope you fare better.

End scene.

I ran the numbers again and you were right: it would be more cost effective to retrofit the Beta with lenses shipped from New York rather than having them made in-country. I'm going to have Mindy make some arrangements and get the details to you.

Lou mentioned that a position with the Geneva labs might be available soon. She asked me if I'd be interested in it and I said yes, so we won't be stuck trading letters like antebellum lovers bent on flouting societal norms. I mean, we can't be ruined if we are willing, right? Okay, I blame you for the way I'm talking. You made me read that romance book, and let me tell you something. It was damn good.

I got you the next one. Check your email.

—A

P.S. If you're up for it, I want to take you to dinner when I get to Geneva. My treat, but you get to pick the spot, so think big.

Grace tapped her fingers on the table and leaned back in her chair. She had just wandered in from a night out, and the warm buzz of the liquor she'd enjoyed hummed in her veins. It was a cool 3 am in Geneva, which meant it was 10 pm or so in New York. She sighed and stretched, glancing at the timestamp on the email—twenty-two minutes ago.

That meant if she replied, like she really wanted to, she'd most likely get a response.

But should she do that, after so many gin and tonics?

Talking to Anton always made her...feel a certain type of way. A certain type of way which was in violation of more than one workplace rule. They were friends, yes, but they did work together, even if they'd never *seen* each other. For six months all of their communication had been through emails and phone calls. And those phone calls had only just begun in the last few weeks. No face-to-face for them, unless you counted the one time she'd wandered into a room while he was on a pixelated video call with her boss and best friend Lou. Grace only had time to shove a bagel into Lou's mouth before her attention had been pulled away by a dustup between the other scientists in response to a shortage of non-latex gloves, but that was all part of her gig as lab manager.

Grace ran the lab as the head lab assistant, or Lab Queen as she preferred, to Louane Wright, world-renowned astrophysicist and her best friend. Their friendship had sprung from mutual need when Grace had taken up the mantle of lab assistant three years earlier. Once mocked for her work on the space-time continuum, Lou became lauded as a pioneer in her field and awarded a research appointment at CERN in Switzerland. She hadn't hesitated for a second in bringing Grace along for the ride.

It had been a dream come true. Everything had fallen into place for Grace since coming to Geneva with Lou—well, until Anton.

He just...didn't fit in with her carefully ordered world.

Her eyes dropped to the *A*, and she sighed, swinging back and forth in her roller chair. She shouldn't even be up right now. Replying wasn't the smartest idea, not when she *knew* Anton would write back, and she only had three hours before she needed to be up.

It wouldn't be the first time she'd lost sleep over chatting with Anton. The pair had begun corresponding because of work and, at first, the emails had been three or four lines at most, counting a thank-you and goodbye. But somewhere in those early emails on specifications for lens delivery and schematic requests Grace and Anton had fallen into a friendly back-and-forth.

She didn't know when it happened, but maybe it had

been inevitable from the start. He was funny, there was no denying it, and he thought she was clever, which only stoked her excitement at seeing a new email appear from *A*, as he signed his emails.

Anton Kovalev.

Grace didn't even need to google him to know who he was. His notoriety preceded him, and from the beginning she had known who she was talking to, on account of the fact that he was famous. Like the big-time kind of famous that demanded nondescript hoodies and dark baseball caps pulled down low over aviator sunglasses to keep people from recognizing him.

It was what happened when you were born a billionaire and frittered away your youth as a hell-raising playboy. Not that any of that mattered in the grand scheme of things, or so Grace told herself.

There was no way the man she knew now was the same one who favored supermodels and sports cars. Her Anton, the one she knew, was one of the leading lights of the science world. He didn't even go home from the labs some nights, opting to sleep on the pull-out couch he kept for just that purpose.

She knew as much because of the phone calls.

She rubbed her neck, thinking back three weeks to that first 2 am call that had woken her up like a jolt of lightning. He'd called four times in the days that followed it, and each time it made her nervous and giddy because those damned sporadic phone calls did far more for her than any date with a man had in months—hell, maybe even years.

She winced, recalling how good his voice sounded

when roughened by sleepiness, how interested he was in her day and her thoughts, even as he chastised her that she should be sleeping.

"If that isn't the pot calling the kettle black," she retorted with a yawn.

"I'd have a snappy comeback, but I like you talking to me."

"Shut up and tell me about your day."

And then he would, and it was pretty much the best part of Grace's day, which was saying something. She got to work beside her best friend, she got to live in a gorgeous city, she was independent, and she was surrounded by a fantastic, if harried, group of scientists she thought of as *hers*. And in some way, Anton was part of that—hers—even if it was only through exchanged emails and the odd phone call.

It was nice. It was theirs and it was—well, she'd take it. Except now there was an invitation to dinner, and Grace didn't know how to process that. Did he mean it as friends? Surely he did...but what if he didn't?

She swallowed hard, rubbing her eyes and blinking at the too-bright screen in the dark of her bedroom.

This was not what she should be doing at this hour. She should be asleep, unconcerned about said dinner invitation until she could run it by Lou. Her best friend would know what Anton meant. After all, they'd been friends for longer than Grace and Anton, so that had to count for something, didn't it?

It wasn't professional. You didn't internet stalk and drool over someone who was supposed to be your work friend.

She shut off her computer to avoid the temptation of

googling Anton and shuffled off to bed with a groan. She needed sleep if she had any hope of controlling the labs for the full twelve hours required of her. Now was not the time to be thinking of Anton, or his smooth-as-silk voice, or the fact he had bought her the second in the romance series she had been obsessing over.

Throwing herself into her bed, she groaned when her mind strayed to what she could remember of his face from all those years ago when she'd seen him in a magazine. Dark brown hair, dark eyes, of that she was sure—but what else? He was tallish? Or maybe not? In possession of two arms and legs?

She couldn't remember anymore.

She frowned at herself for her less than helpful recollection of Anton's appearance. How damn frustrating. This was going to bother her like a half-remembered lyric looping through her memory. She was certain there was at least one documented case of a person going insane from just such a thing.

She yanked the pillow over her head with a grunt and muttered, "Serves you right. You shouldn't even be thinking like this. Go to sleep—you're drunk."

She closed her eyes and forced herself to lay still. Any thoughts of Anton were pushed away, G&T buzz be damned. She wasn't going to reply to his email. She wasn't going to google him, she wasn't going to call him or stay up hoping that he would call *her.* What she was going to do was get some kind of sleep so that she could function in the morning.

She was a grown woman, in command of her thoughts and libido.

He didn't even know what she looked like, for Odin's sake. There was no way he had asked her out on a date.

No way at all. Not even a tiny bit. Absolutely not.

Anton Kovalev was *not asking her out.*

Grace achieved zero sleep that night.

CHAPTER ONE

"I HAVE NO IDEA. People who boast about their I.Q. are losers."
—Stephen Hawking

GRACE KNEW she tempted gravity by balancing a triple-stacked tray of coffees which resembled the Leaning Tower of Pisa, but she didn't give a whit.

Time was of the essence, with cold hard physics and steaming cups of caffeine on the line. Gravity be damned. There were sleepy physicists to caffeinate. Shifting the coffees and the bag full of bagels in her other hand, she kicked the door to the lab open and swept in with all the gravitas of a returning hero.

Chaos had erupted during her quick jaunt to get breakfast for her science tribe. Sighing, Grace took in the scene before she sprang into action, executing the fine art of science-wrangling. Caring for cosmos-obsessed geniuses was her art form of choice.

That, and overthinking.

Grace began to dole out coffee and bagels to caffeine-starved hands when she heard a shout from her favorite astrophysics genius.

"Gracie?"

Lou shoved her way out from behind a lab table and made a beeline for Grace.

"Morning, boss lady," Grace chirped, offering a cup of coffee to the smaller woman.

"Please tell me that's coffee."

"Verily." Grace gave the cup a little wiggle. An excited moan escaped Lou's mouth before she took the cup.

"You're my favorite lab assistant," she said, looking at the bagel Grace thrust into her free hand.

"I'm your only lab assistant."

"No, you aren't." Lou took a quick bite of the bagel and gestured around the lab with it. "Look at this. We're in the big-time now."

"All because of your big science brain, Lou," Grace said, still only half-believing that her job was to hang out with her best friend and tag-team the mysteries of the universe. She hustled to complete her morning march through the lab space, handing out breakfast as she went. The sooner she fed her science tribe, the better the odds that nothing exploded, or ended up launched at top speeds, or got taken apart that should have been left alone.

"Okay, true. But we all know who runs this show," Lou said, taking a healthy bite of her bagel as she trailed after Grace. "Which reminds me. I have someone to introduce you to." She threaded her arm through Grace's and yanked her forward.

"Whoa." Grace dug her heels in to keep upright as her tiny friend marched forward. Lou was no couch potato, but the determined set to her small shoulders and the firm grip on Grace's arm set off alarm bells in her head. She hoped Lou wasn't trying to set her up again—a hobby that the astrophysicist managed to indulge in despite a full schedule of exploding, launching, and cosmos-searching.

"Who are we meeting? I swear to god, Lou, if this is another set-up I'll run straight out of here so fast," Grace hissed in her friend's ear, but Lou rolled her eyes.

"As much as I love meddling in your love life, this isn't that," Lou said, giving Grace another yank. "Anton Kovalev is here. Isn't that exciting? You finally get to meet him." Her friend bounced along, but Grace bit her lip.

"Umm...he's coming this week?"

Lou narrowed her eyes. "Have you just not been reading the emails I forwarded to you? I sent them to you to read up on this weekend. You know how much he's been helping us get this project done, Gracie. This is important."

Grace nodded, mind flying to the email Anton had sent her a few days before. She'd meant to read it; there was the fact that she still wasn't sure if he had asked her out on a date, which had become a bigger possibility and also a massive occasion to embarrass herself if she'd misunderstood—so rather than reply she'd simply...pushed it off to the side.

Out of sight, out of mind, and all that.

"Yeah, about that..." she hedged, pulling at an imaginary collar that felt too snug under the shrewd gaze of her best friend.

How could she bring up the maybe-date to her now?

She couldn't. Plain and simple.

"What do you mean, *about that*?"

"I—" Grace lifted one shoulder in a shrug, eyes sliding to the side. "Okay, it's not that I don't read them, per se." She made a show of looking at her nails as they walked.

"Anton Kovalev is one of the most brilliant astrophysicists of—oh, I don't know—forever," Lou exploded, earning a feigned blank-eyed look from Grace. Of course she knew that, but she maintained her poker face as Lou huffed at her. Lou crossed her arms and tried again. "You love reality television and gossip rags, so let's look at it this way. If the physics world did a 30 under 30, he'd be on it."

Grace unholstered not one but two finger guns and pointed them at her friend. "See, to me, that's you. And besides, I know who he is. He's my friend too, you know."

The other woman narrowed her eyes and smacked her fingers away, a treatment Grace endured because she didn't have the fortitude to admit the reason she hadn't read the emails was because of an avoidance-related front-flip into a reality television binge session. She winced, thinking about how she still hadn't emailed him back.

Real smooth.

If it *had* been a date, it probably wasn't by now.

"Stop buttering up to me to make me forget you didn't read the emails I forwarded you."

"Can't blame me for trying."

"Anyhow," Lou said, giving her a withering look before continuing, "he's amazing, not to mention the brain behind all the retrofitting we've been doing on the Beta telescope—"

"Her name is Betsy," Grace said with an indignant sniff on behalf of the infrared telescope on which all their hopes and dreams rode.

Once an outdated piece of engineering, the old refractor telescope, the last of its kind, had been repurposed for Lou's research. It was no small secret that the telescope's leap to using cutting-edge technology was a wild card in Lou's hand she'd leveraged to have free reign in her labs and with CERN resources.

Lou's research was brilliant in how it examined black hole behavior and pulsar waves to tag gravitational anomalies, but that didn't mean Lou would have been able to land her spot without a scientist like Anton Kovalev backing their research.

Grace's mind strayed to that one time she'd glimpsed Anton in a pixelated and choppy video call on her way in and out of Lou's office, when she'd forced the other woman to eat, as she so often had to do. She didn't need to be thinking of how he looked. She needed to be thinking of how to best integrate his team with hers. How she could help him settle in, and what kind of access to Betsy he was going to need.

Not...whatever it was that her mind and body did when the topic of Anton came up.

Grace owed him for helping them get their foot in the door, and for taking on the project of bringing their telescope into this century. None of it would have been possible without him. She would have to make his stay a happy one to show her thanks.

The man deserved the royal treatment, not ogling.

Lou rolled her eyes. "I think you mean Beta."

"Look, she deserves a *real* name."

"It's a telescope, Gracie. It doesn't need a name."

Grace shrugged and held up her hands. "She's gonna do big things, and Beta isn't exactly a name to write home about."

"And Betsy is?"

Grace grinned. "Totally. It's the name of a cranky old woman, which she is."

Lou laughed and shook her head. "You can call her Betsy all you want, but I'm not. And," she said, holding up a finger, "neither is Anton or any of his team, so keep your scheming to yourself. I'm excited about him being here in Geneva with us. We've been collaborating for so long, and now he's here, so we can leave those god-awful video calls behind."

"That's great." Grace rubbed her hands together. "Where is he? I can't wait to add another scientist to my roster."

"He's just getting acquainted with the tech and, Gracie, you're gonna love him."

Grace blushed. It wasn't that she hadn't told Lou about their emails and how friendly they'd gotten, but she might have left out the fact that they'd begun calling each other, which was fine because it wasn't a big deal.

Not really. Just a tiny deal.

"I mean, I know you guys get on well in email, but Anton is just wonderful! Really and truly a wonderful guy

—I can't tell you how nice it's been talking over things with an actual human and— Holy shit, what are they doing?" Lou's eyes widened as she caught sight of what appeared to be a poor recreation of *West Side Story* starring her team of physicists.

"That was *my* coffee," a wild-eyed physicist yelled, breaking ranks from the others. "Don't act like you didn't know, Karen."

"Oh god, the unrest," Grace muttered as Lou huffed and bustled past her.

"I'll put this one down. Just give me a sec." Lou charged off, but not before snatching a sharpie off the table next to them.

The move intrigued Grace. What did Lou intend to do, armed with a single sharpie? She had taken her first step toward the fray when someone tapped her on the shoulder.

"Coffee. Black."

That voice was—suffice it to say that it was a lovely voice, all smoothness with a rich timbre that sent Grace's stomach into a somersault.

It was also...*familiar*.

She swore she'd heard it before, but then it had made her feel at home—relaxed—hadn't it?

If only it weren't dictating a coffee order to her like a drive-thru menu at Starbucks. She was a woman in her prime, for god sake, not a speaker box.

Grace whirled around and raised an eyebrow. "Excuse me?"

Looking back at her was a man she had never seen before, a fact Grace lamented because Mr. Mystery Man looked like he had just walked off the set of some photo-shoot. That or a romance novel cover, the sort to feature a scoundrel for the modern age.

He was a masterpiece composed of sensuous lips and eyes capable of hypnotizing a woman into parting with her PIN for her bank card. Dark unruly hair fell over his forehead in a manner she suspected took far more styling and preparation than he would ever let on.

Always a sucker for brunettes, she itched to run her fingers through his hair, a move she was sure would destroy his coif.

He wore a knee-length camel wool coat with a turned-up collar, a thick black turtleneck, and joggers. She didn't miss the luxurious black leather of the man's combat boots, into which his joggers had been tucked. He looked at ease, styled to be cozy, walking the line between trendy and classic. His warm whiskey-colored eyes, high cheek-bones, scruff-covered jaw so sharp she was convinced it could be considered a weapon by the TSA, and sun-kissed skin demanded her attention. He was everything she looked for in a lover.

At least, he would have been, if not for the look in his eyes.

Dismissive.

The pulse at the base of her throat began to accelerate, but not in the sexy fun-time kind of way.

He sighed at her question, eyes already dropping down to the cell phone in his hand. "Coffee. Now."

"What's the magic word?" she shot back with narrowed eyes. Grace wasn't just a sucker for brunettes, but also assholes. Always assholes. If there was a man in possession of questionable mores, terrible communication skills, and nonexistent concern for others, she couldn't help but be drawn to him.

She should have known Mystery Man was cut from that particular type of undesirable dishcloth.

Now it was his turn to gape, and he looked up from the cell phone screen he had already deemed more important than her. "Excuse me?" he asked, parroting her.

And again that rush of familiarity hit her over the head like a metal chair in a cage match.

She had heard this voice before. She knew it. Was he a voice actor? An insufferably snotty voice actor?

"I said," she reiterated, crossing her arms and tossing her hair over her shoulder, "what's the magic word?" The entitled look on his face was enough to make her blood boil. She could tell this was a man not used to encountering defiance, and she stood a little taller, glad to give him a taste of his own medicine.

"Look, why don't you do your job and get me some coffee?" He ran a hand, a hand she hated noticing for being long fingered and well-formed, across his jaw as he stared at her. His hands looked more than capable of all manner of things, callused as they were in a curious juxtaposition to his curated ensemble.

So sue her, she had a thing for men's hands, and this man, for all his rudeness, had beautiful specimens she wouldn't mind knowing behind closed doors if she didn't want to slap him into the next lunar cycle. Her fingers twitched at the thought.

"My job?" she asked, unable to keep the shrill tone out of her voice. "Who the hell even let you in here?"

"Yes, your job," he said with an incredulous toss of his head. "Coffee. N—"

"Don't you dare say *now*, you—you..." she spluttered.

"You what?" he asked, taking a step closer to her with a smirk that showed he enjoyed pushing her buttons.

How dare he think he could order her around like this? If she hit him over the head with the nearest science instrument, she figured that no court of law would hold her accountable. Not with this treatment.

No matter that she walked a fine line between wanting to slap him and kiss him. Physical attraction could be so inconvenient sometimes.

He winked at her. "Come on, sweetie. Use your words."

The audacity.

"You *brat*," she exploded.

The man's eyebrows shot up, and he was silent for a beat before he threw his head back and laughed. Much to her consternation, it wasn't just any laugh; it was a full-body, from-his-belly kind of laugh.

He had a nice laugh. It made her angrier. A man who acted like he did had no right possessing the sort of laugh capable of warming her down to her toes.

"I don't see what's so funny. You're behaving like an ass. No, not even that, you straightened-out wire coat hanger! You're—"

"Hey! *No!*" Lou yelled, appearing at her elbow. She shook an uncapped sharpie at Grace in a way that reminded her Lou had just ended a scuffle with naught but the simple marker.

"Don't *no* me," Grace yelled back, taking a sidestep away from her sharpie-wielding friend.

"Then don't call Anton an ass or—" She paused and gave Grace a perplexed look. "A straightened-out wire coat hanger? I mean, why?"

Anton.

That one word brought Grace's world crashing down around her with the force of an atomic explosion.

It was him. He was here. The snotty voice actor was *her* Anton.

It hadn't even crossed her mind, not with the entitled manner he'd spoken to her, not when he had treated her like nothing.

Her Anton didn't do that—*wouldn't.* And yet here he was, doing just that.

Grace jabbed a finger at the boorish man she had just been tempted to slap. "The broken coat hanger is Anton? There's no way."

"The one and only." Anton put one hand on his chest before giving her a low bow, complete with a flourish of his other hand. "Anton Kovalev."

Grace frowned, thinking back to the phone calls, the emails, the fluttering sensation in her stomach associated with the name Anton. How could *he* be the man who still bowed, though now he looked up at her with an infuriating smile?

His face, Grace decided, was stupid, but only because she wanted to dart forward and kiss the smile right off it.

That would show him some manners.

Of course this was Anton, who turned out to be an

asshole in person. *Of course* she had fallen for him without letting herself google search him.

Of course, of course, of course.

"He isn't nice," she blurted out, giving Lou a sidelong look. "At all. Not even a tiny bit." She glared and shook a finger at him. "You—you're supposed to be nice. I expected courteous and kind, maybe even a little cheeky, but not a demanding prima donna!"

Lou sighed. "Look—"

"I still need a coffee," Anton interrupted, uprighting himself and leaning against the back of a lab table.

He looked bored with what was going on in front of him, and Grace decided she would rather walk over broken telescope lenses or get lost in the curvature of time and space for the rest of her natural life before she got the man a single thing.

She cared for her science tribe out of the goodness of her heart, out of her desire to see them grow up to be healthy, strong science minions. She'd thought of this man as hers, but now she knew that'd been a mistake.

The whole stupid thing, thoughts of a date with him included, had been a terrible mistake. This man was not one of her brood, and she fixed him with a caustic glare.

"You'll get nothing and like it, buster."

Lou dropped the sharpie with a gasp at Grace's vehemence. She had never known her friend to speak like that to anyone, but here Grace was, staring down one of the most brilliant physics minds in the world, fire in her eyes.

"What the hell happened? I was gone for two minutes." Lou's eyes darted between the pair, who were now locked in a battle of stares.

"Says who?" Anton asked Grace, ignoring Lou's question. "A glorified delivery girl?"

"Anton!" Lou's eyes widened in shock at the other astrophysicist, but Grace had drawn herself up to her full height and stared down the man in front of her. If he thought he could talk to her like that and get away unscathed, he was mistaken. She wasn't Grace Muñoz, Queen of Overthinking and Science Geniuses, for nothing.

"A delivery girl? That's rich, coming from a Steve Jobs rip-off!"

She felt a measure of satisfaction course through her when Anton's face flushed, and he shook his head, running a hand through his hair.

"Real original. The man didn't corner the market on a good turtleneck."

"You *would* say that."

"Why would I say that?"

"Because right now you're the mayor of Turtleneck Town."

"What the—Turtleneck Town?" Anton shook his head and gave her a look that suggested he questioned her sanity. "What are you? Five?"

Grace rolled her eyes. "Says the man lacking basic etiquette. Just because you're in here looking all European chic and windswept doesn't give you the right to—"

"You think I'm chic?" Anton asked with a quirk of his mouth.

"That—hey, that is not what's on trial here."

"It's not?" He pushed himself away from the lab table

and took a slow sauntering step toward her. "Windswept, was it?"

"No, you stop that. Don't think I don't know what you're trying to do with those bedroom eyes. We are talking about your abhorrent treatment of people. I thought you were better than this."

He rubbed a hand along his jaw and gave her a smirk. "And what would give you reason to believe that? You don't even know me."

Grace's eyes widened like she'd been slapped. He didn't know who she was. Hadn't realized it. She could tell from his flippant tone that he had no clue it was her, his friend, the one he bought books for and invited to dinner.

Or maybe he knew and just didn't care.

She couldn't say because this Anton wasn't the one she'd known.

Lou's eyes darted between the couple, who appeared poised to swing pieces of her custom equipment at one another—though a part of her couldn't help but wonder at the too-bright look in Anton's eyes, or the flush on Gracie's cheeks, not to mention the fact that the couple's pupils were full-blown dilated. The physical reactions on their own were suspect, but taken together they resembled arousal far too closely for her to ignore.

Lou had to stop them, lest she end up with Anton throwing Grace down on a lab table while her beloved assistant smashed him over the head with a microscope.

With time of the essence, Lou did the only sensible thing she could think of and snatched up the first thing near her, a spray bottle full of distilled water. Bottle in hand, she sprayed the pair down, much like her grandmother did her horde of cats when they took to fighting.

The bickering pair didn't notice the first spritz of water, but it only took a few squeezes for them to freeze and turn in sync toward Lou, who held the spray bottle like it was a revolver. She squeezed the pump again when Grace opened her mouth and blinked.

"Are you really spraying us down with water?" Grace bit her lip and tried not to notice how long Anton's eyelashes were now that his face was covered in a fine mist.

"You gave me no choice," Lou said, and shook the bottle at them. "Now make up or I'll empty this whole damn thing on you."

"You wouldn't dare." Anton's hands went to his hips.

"Try me, Kovalev."

"She's serious," Grace muttered, holding up her hands in surrender. "I'm sorry that this...neanderthal—"

"I think the record shows I am a European-chic, windswept neanderthal," Anton interrupted with a grin that nearly made Grace growl. She found her dislike of the man made her almost vibrate with frustration. His amusement at the situation just made it worse.

Not to mention, it was a bullshit move by the universe that Anton was so handsome. Why couldn't the handsome ones be nice? Did that ever happen in real life, or was it just the sugar-sweet opiate Hollywood sold her by the bucketful?

Alas, there weren't fated meet-cutes, or beautiful gentlemen capable of actual human manners eager to sweep her off her feet. Just demanding astrophysicist assholes with stupid pretty faces.

Grace frowned, glaring at Anton's picture-perfect hair, but when he raised an eyebrow at her expression, she glanced back at Lou.

"I'm sorry. I apologize," Anton said, his voice low and husky in a tone that Grace bet worked to get him out of trouble whenever the need called for it. He looked at Lou with soulful brown eyes that held none of the disdain they had when he'd demanded coffee from Grace.

Lou's face softened at Anton's words, but Grace didn't believe the man for an instant. She was on to this pretty trickster's games. He had fooled her in his emails and made her tenderhearted with a few phone calls.

This man was a Liar McLiarson, and that was that.

She snorted her displeasure at his apology, but a warning look from Lou had her falling quiet.

"I'm sorry, too," Grace sighed, looking down at the floor...anywhere but at Anton.

He glowed with pleasure beside her, and she wasn't sure if she wanted to throw herself at him or maim him. She pursed her lips when she caught herself daydreaming of his capable hands and the husky tone he'd infused his voice with.

Perhaps it was a bit of both? So sue her, she was only human. Just because she was convinced she hated him didn't mean Anton wasn't easy to look at. If anything, it only heightened her awareness of him. Demanded that she not let her guard down around him again, like she had before.

"Good." Lou nodded at them and cleared her throat.

"Now that we've got that drama settled, I'll show you around, Anton." She met Grace's gaze with her own. "You'll be all right?"

Grace prickled at the question, but only because she knew Anton paid close attention to her, and she could just imagine what the man thought a "glorified delivery girl" would do when left in charge of a physics lab.

"Of course. I'm working with David and Bruce on the readings we pulled last night. I'll have them cross-referenced with the previous two data sets and see if we can pick up any new activity. If we're not here when you get back, then we've gone to see Betsy."

Grace did her utmost not to give in to the rush of pleasure at the appraising look Anton gave her. He seemed to be reconsidering her.

Grace looked away, refusing to give him a second more of her attention. Only under the duress of a bonafide waterboarding session would she admit how she felt a tiny bit of—okay, no, a humongous Taco Tuesday's worth of—satisfaction at turning his perception of her on its head.

Not that it mattered.

Anton's opinion of her was inconsequential. He wasn't who she'd thought he was, and that was that. Just because she found him attractive—okay, were rakish and handsome permissible descriptors if he wasn't sporting a cravat on the cover of a historical romance novel? She voted yes, because that was what this man looked like to her, for all of his dismissive behavior.

All that he lacked was a pair of tight breeches, some landed gentry as background characters, and a swooning heroine to complete the picture. She glanced at him then, meeting those soulful eyes trained on her, and inclined her head to him before she wiggled her fingers goodbye to Lou.

She was not volunteering as tribute for the role of swooning heroine.

Not now.

Not ever.

That ship had sailed the second he'd talked to her like she didn't matter.

What Grace did have, however, was a metric ton of coffee to drink and science to do, both of which outranked the opinion of a mannerless urchin, no matter how fine his hands were, or how windswept he looked.

CHAPTER TWO

"Two things are infinite: the universe and human stupidity; and I'm not sure about the universe."

—Albert Einstein

"Stupid," Anton muttered. He was in his temporary home for his stay in Geneva, a chic hotel only a short walk away from the labs. Since he had returned to his penthouse suite, he'd been pacing nonstop, wearing a path into the carpeting. The day's events played nonstop on the IMAX screen that was his brain.

What had he been thinking?

How had he not realized it was Grace?

Even if it hadn't been, his behavior was so out of line it was almost laughable. He winced, turning away from the window, and yanked at his hair in frustration.

He stalked over to the windows overlooking the cityscape. There had been no reason for his poor showing that afternoon...well, nothing other than his piss-poor mood at having his latest schematics stolen.

During his time at MIT, Anton had spent a good portion of his education focused on enhancing the ability of modern telescopes to examine the vastness of the cosmos. Time and space were mysteries that fascinated him, so it came as little surprise that after his graduation he had devoted himself and the resources of his sizeable fortune to improving and testing the boundaries of what telescopes could do.

The stolen schematic had been the product of three years of labor, and the loss had sent Anton to a dark place, a place he hadn't visited since enrolling in MIT, not since his more...colorful days. The infrared spectrograph he had affectionately dubbed RED should have allowed his company—KovT, or Kovalev Technologies—to examine thousands of galaxies...and not just that, but the *earliest* galaxies.

RED was the key to looking at the beginning of everything. The tech was amazing, and goddamned groundbreaking...but then the unthinkable had happened. RED had been stolen, and after a panicked twenty-four hours it had reappeared as BLUE and in the hands of Orion Star, Anton's greatest nemesis—you know, if astrophysics had that sort of thing.

Turned out Anton did.

It had been an absolute field day when the press had scrambled from the loss of Anton's tech to the curious announcement of similar tech. There was talk of a mole, of a sticky-fingered bandit, that made Anton grit his teeth in press conferences.

One of the questions had proved just too much for Anton to grin and bear in silence.

"Are you dating any new supermodels?"

"Excuse me?" Anton's jaw had clenched so tight it would be a wonder if he had even a single tooth left that hadn't been reduced to something resembling protein powder.

The reporter who had asked the question wavered under his intense stare but forged ahead with impressive confidence. "Are you dating any new supermodels?" they repeated.

"How does that have anything to do with RED?"

Anton had leaned back in his chair. He could feel his blood pressure skyrocketing, and he forced his body to adopt an apathetic pose. He deserved an Oscar for not throttling the reporter.

It never failed, no matter how much he did for science, how many charities he founded or donated to, or how many scholarships he created. At the slightest hint of a scandal, the public was all too eager to forget all the good he'd done, especially when there was a juicy rumor afoot, and especially considering his past.

Anton had forced his expression to pure boredom and glanced down at his nails as he waited for the reporter to answer. There was a beat of deafening silence before they cleared their throat and spoke.

"Well, isn't it true that you named the telescope for Amelia Corins?"

Anton looked up from his nails with a raised eyebrow. "Who?"

"The supermodel, Amelia Corins."

"Never heard of her."

"You were rumored to have been in contac—"

"Why would I name my tech after a supermodel I don't know?" Anton leaned forward and steepled his fingers against his chin.

The reporter shifted, and for the first time looked unsure. "Her red hair?"

Anton cracked a wry smile and turned his face into his hands with a chuckle. "Are you serious?"

"Y-yes?" The reporter swallowed hard and looked like they wanted to be anywhere but here, with the eyes of the packed room trained on them.

"My team and I develop technology capable of examining the first galaxies in existence, and you think I named it after a woman's hair color? We just lost millions of dollars of development, and that's where you go?" Anton put his hands down flat on the conference table and leveled a glare at the reporter.

"It was speculated when you unveiled the name and—"

"Do you know what infrared is? Ever heard of it? Red is an abbreviation for it."

The reporter cleared their throat. "I see that now—"

"The next time one of you brings up a supermodel in these conferences, I walk. In fact," Anton said, standing from his table with a jerk, "I'm leaving now. I have a flight to catch. It's been a pleasure."

The room had erupted in a flurry of voices, all of them wanting to know his next move, where his flight was going, if he was going to sue Orion Star—but Anton didn't pause in his march toward the conference door or answer a single question.

Instead, he blew the roomful of reporters a number of air kisses.

It was all he could do to not howl in frustration; once again, his youthful antics had overshadowed the honest to goodness real science he had conducted. At least the air kisses were the perfect gesture to distract from the debilitating loss of RED.

The press still expected him to behave like a childish playboy, so that was what he gave them.

If only to keep them distracted long enough to make a getaway.

Only those in the science community would understand, and that was why his inbox hadn't stopped pinging with condolences over RED's theft. Each message had come with an invitation. But his thoughts had only gone to one person he wanted to discuss his loss with: Grace.

The precious few phone calls he'd exchanged with her had become treasured moments for him to find respite in. A conversation with Grace had a way of shifting Anton's perspective, making him re-examine what was important.

He'd meant to call her, but things had snowballed until he found himself buried beneath well wishes and offers of assistance.

Some offered him a place to lay low on a beach in South America, or even France; there had been an invitation to do a bit of Formula One racing in Brazil, a particularly tempting thought.

However, the most alluring invite of them all had come before his sudden need to disappear. He'd been considering it for weeks, had only just gotten up the courage to tell Grace about it a few days ago, in fact.

He had spent far too much time daydreaming about his science pen pal than was healthy. If he were honest he'd admit it was by far the most attractive perk of all the places he could run to. Why he'd waited two weeks to act on it he didn't know, but he was grateful all the same for the offer from his-longtime-until-then-FaceTime-friend Lou Wright, who promised him a lab to work and play in, at CERN of all places.

The timing couldn't have been more perfect for an utterly imperfect scenario.

For nearly a year, Lou and Anton had worked together on rehauling a telescope that should have been retired at least two decades before. Calling it obsolete was being kind. When Lou had reached out to him about ideas to improve it so she could use it for her research, Anton had hesitated, but then he'd learned what Lou and her ragtag band of scientists were trying to do.

Prove gravity functioned as a wave—and not just prove it, but predict its behavior.

It was ambitious but doable with the right minds and resources. Intrigued, Anton had agreed to a video call with the diminutive astrophysicist, and by the end of it he had not only been impressed by her passion for the field but he'd come to respect her tenacity.

It was no secret Lou Wright had been all but blackballed early in her career by the "old guard" of gentleman scholars who found her claims a tad too fanciful. Anton wasn't fooled; he knew the woman intimidated them, which motivated them to push her to the fringes of the science community.

And for all of those reasons Anton hadn't hesitated to

help Lou or lend his resources to her cause. He would help her rebuild the grandest telescope in the hemisphere. If her research failed, it wouldn't be for the want of technology.

In light of RED's theft and Anton's sudden urge to leave New York City far behind, the decision to join Lou for some hands-on work retrofitting the telescope had been a no-brainer. Now Anton was the one indebted to Lou for the little slice of heaven she had offered him.

Afterward, he'd packed a carry-on, dangled a trip to Geneva in front of his team of science worker bees, found a copy of the *New York Times* with his face plastered across the front of it, and gone on his not-so-merry-way.

Eight hours and just as many pity cocktails later, Anton had shuffled from the airport to the waiting town-car, and against his better judgment made a beeline straight to Lou's labs. Why he'd done that and not opted for rest or caffeine he didn't know. At the very least he could have sobered up. He'd always been a bit of a lush, and old habits were hard to break, even when one became an astrophysicist.

Suffice it to say Anton had been in a deplorable state when he'd set foot in the labs. He supposed that eight undisturbed hours of brooding over being robbed blind did that to a man.

Not that it excused his terrible treatment of Grace.

How he had managed to do what he'd done and to *her*, to *Grace*, left him flabbergasted. Had he even changed from the man he'd once been if he could talk to a perfect stranger like he had?

"A delivery girl..." Anton rubbed a hand over his jaw

and let his forehead hit the window with a thunk. "You're a real charmer, Kovalev," he sighed at himself.

That morning, he'd known he was being an absolute beast when he'd barked his order at the woman, but he'd done it anyhow, like a child. He had deserved every roll of her eyes and sharp word she'd tossed his way—well, except for her dig at his turtleneck.

Anton fingered the collar of his sweater with a frown. The black turtleneck was classic, fashionable, and travel-appropriate.

Damn it all, he had put in the work to turn into someone who was good, patient, and more than capable of treating strangers well, no matter their job titles. And even if his hard work had been stolen and he'd had a long, boozy flight, there was no excuse for his behavior.

Pushing away from the window, Anton walked back over to his bed and fell back onto it with a groan. His thoughts refused to turn from the pretty, smart-mouthed assistant.

She was his friend.

Had been his friend?

He didn't know anymore.

"Grace," he said, testing the name and hating that he liked the way it sounded in the quiet room. She'd been a sight for sore eyes, nevermind the fact that he'd never seen her before aside from a pixelated wave of an arm while she shoved carbs into Lou's mouth. Something in him had sat up and taken notice when she'd turned to face him with her flashing brown eyes, which Anton was certain could be described as lovely even if she had been glaring at him. She'd been calm and steely, even with his attitude.

As much as Anton hated his own behavior, he'd just as much been aroused by Grace's display of backbone.

Anton sighed, fingers drumming against the glass of the window as he thought back to that first phone call—the one that had let him know he was well and truly fucked when it came to his email pen pal.

"Hello?" she'd answered in a breathy voice that had simultaneously struck him stupid and made him feel capable of number theory with nothing but his fingers and toes.

She was electrifying.

Getting to know Grace had made him grateful that he'd become someone decent. And yet...he had managed to show her the worst part of himself. Like time had rewound back to the idiot he'd been six years ago and not the person he had worked hard to become. Anton should be sitting with her now at the dinner he'd asked her to.

The vague date he had asked her on.

Well, *sort of* asked her out on.

Blowing out a sigh, he let his forehead drop forward against the window, and he frowned. He'd been charming once, smooth by all accounts, and entirely capable of making a woman's knees weak. There were entire articles dedicated to documenting his previous dating ways and his effect on women, for crying out loud. But all of that previous experience and debonair attitude had evaporated right up when he'd clumsily asked Grace to dinner.

He must have read over that quick one line dozens of times before he'd hit send, and then poured himself more whiskey than he should have to slow the beating of his heart.

Grace excited him but she made him nervous too. The possibility of rejection had been a constant fear—even sight unseen, Anton had known she was the kind of woman he wanted in his life in a capacity far more intimate than email pen pal.

He groaned, eyes squeezing shut. Now he had begun thinking about just how gorgeous she was. Faceless, Grace was intoxicating, but now that he'd seen her?

He was hopeless. He didn't stand a chance.

He was a mess. A smitten mess.

Grace challenged him, and her sharp mind had him coming back for more, *wanting* more from her. But on top of that she *had* to be gorgeous, didn't she? Her heart-shaped mouth and lush curves made him want to touch her all over and not stop until...well, he didn't want to stop, ever.

And then there was her hair, that mass of bright bubblegum pink that had nearly stopped him in his tracks despite his angry mood. Anton hadn't known that Grace had pink hair. She'd never mentioned it in their talks, but then again, why would she have? The unexpected color was just like her.

Bold. Surprising. Lovely.

It suited her *perfectly*.

Grace's hair had been pulled back into a thick ponytail that fell down the length of her back. The vibrant color suited her dark eyes and accentuated her tan skin in a way that made him think of summer nights and the Fourth of July.

Not to mention her smell was intoxicating. When she'd drawn close to tell him off, he'd struggled to stop from leaning in and breathing in her cinnamon scent. He didn't know if it was her perfume or if she'd just eaten a damn cinnamon roll that morning, but the effect was mouth-watering.

Anton grimaced. Grace, his friend, was as gorgeous as she was unexpected. She was going to be distracting, of that he was certain. Even if he managed to repair their relationship, he didn't see a future in which he was able to work peacefully with the dark-eyed beauty.

Her pink hair alone was going to be an instant flag to pull his attention away from his work. The cinnamon and sugar smell of her would inevitably leave him a mess. God forbid, he was done in by the sway in her ample hips.

Anton closed his eyes, head thunking against the window in front of him again as he felt his skin warm at the pretty little picture Grace had made that morning, all curves, hips, and ass enticingly moving as she walked, the sinful outline of her perky breasts against her white t-shirt. Her tawny skin looked so smooth and soft, and those pillowy lips of hers begged to be kissed. His instant attraction to her wouldn't have been as bad, or nearly as distracting, if he hadn't noticed her own response to him.

He'd suspected that Grace liked him. Counted on it, in fact, when he'd called her out of the blue those few weeks ago. Had planned to use it to his advantage when he sent her the invitation to dinner.

Today he saw what he'd hoped for.

Grace *did* want him. Want him like he'd wanted her for months. For all his reformed ways, Anton knew he was attractive, and he hadn't missed the way Grace's eyes kept darting to his mouth, his hands—how she'd called him windswept, or told him that he had "bedroom eyes." She had taken just as much notice of him as he had of her, which made the whole situation that much more disastrous.

If he'd been a teensy bit—okay, a terribly large amount—more sober, and hadn't been brooding for eight straight hours beforehand, their first face-to-face meeting might have yielded a far more satisfying interaction. But that hadn't happened, and now he was alone, coping with a terrible hangover, horny over thoughts of her.

"Peachy," he muttered. He moved away from the window, suddenly warmer than was comfortable. His clothes seemed too constricting, and he pulled off his sweater with a jerk. There was no doubt that he was aroused; his flushed skin, the ache in his groin, and the uncharacteristically fast beat of his heart were all telltale signs. He rubbed a hand over his face once more, images of sable eyes and cotton candy pink tresses wreaking havoc on his calm.

Grace was going to be a distraction, alright.

He swallowed hard, flustered at how easily thoughts of the lab assistant left him wanting and out of breath. Christ, he hadn't even spent a day in the labs with her and already his body betrayed him.

"Grace," he said again, and stifled a sigh. He wondered what she was doing, if she was as bothered as he was over their tiff that morning. Was she thinking over their last conversation? Wondering about the dinner invitation and what he had meant? Or...was she onto bigger and more pleasant things? Was she alone as well? The shower, maybe? His cock twitched at the thought and he leapt up from the bed with a wave of his hands.

"No, not going there. Abso-fucking-lutely not." He held his hands up and shook his head at himself. "Shut it down, buddy," he said, glaring at his crotch. The order fell on deaf ears with ever enticing images of her flitting through his mind, and he made a beeline for the bathroom.

"I need a cold shower. No, I need an absolutely arctic drowning."

He kicked off his shoes and shook his head as he yanked off his pants. "I'm not going down like this. I don't care how gorgeous she is, or if she smells like cinnamon rolls on steroids. I am a respected, professional astrophysicist. And that is final. " He nodded at his reflection, but almost groaned at the sight of his tented boxers.

Apparently, his pep talk hadn't done a thing to dampen his lust.

Turning the water to the coldest setting he could bear, he all but flung himself under the freezing stream of water. Only then, with the icy shower all around him, was he able to breathe easier and take full control of his thoughts. Grace was beautiful, she was his type, and she was witty and kind, but she was his friend, or he hoped she would be again when he repaired the damage he'd done. And besides, he hadn't worked as hard as he had to leave behind his reputation as a playboy only to be done in on the first day by her.

Absolutely not happening.

What he did on the second, or even third day, without

the influence of a cold shower, was an entirely different story.

~

"I CANNOT BELIEVE THAT WAS ANTON." Grace flung the hand not holding her glass of wine in the general direction of wherever Anton was in the wild blue yonder. "I feel hoodwinked."

Lou winced. "It was not the best foot for you both to get off on."

Grace rolled her eyes and said nothing, preferring a long swallow of her red wine to letting the scathing remark on her tongue loose. She knew better than to push too much, because even if Lou was her best friend, the woman took her work and her colleagues seriously.

Lou was also loyal to a fault, and she considered Anton and all his bad manners to be her friend. It would only put a damper on the evening if Grace really tore into him.

"I know, I know," Lou said with a nod. "You wouldn't so much as throw a cup of coffee on him if he was on fire."

Grace snorted. "Okay, but to be fair I wouldn't waste good caffeine on anyone like that. I mean, you ever heard of stop, drop, 'n' roll?"

Lou cracked a smile and squeezed Grace's hands. "You know he isn't that kind of man."

"What kind of man is that?"

"The kind who acts like an asshole." Lou leaned forward, giving Grace an earnest look. "He means a great deal to me."

"You mean his big science brain means a great deal to you."

"No, it isn't just that. Anton's my friend, Gracie."

She pulled a face at Lou's declaration. "That's because you're sweet and pure of heart. Everyone is your damn friend," she muttered. She hated that she'd considered him her friend too. That was the worst part of it all. She'd fallen for whatever fake "Nice Guy" routine Anton had given her, only to awaken to the nightmare that the man truly was.

"But you're my favorite." Lou gave their linked hands a little shake, and Grace snapped out of her brooding.

She eyed their hands. "You're buttering me up," she said, dropping her eyes to their hands. If Grace weren't so annoyed at Anton, she would be downright impressed by Lou's blatant exploitation.

"I am," Lou admitted with a wince.

"Why?"

"I need you to be on your best behavior with Anton."

When Grace opened her mouth to protest, Lou gave her a pleading look, one that had the full power of puppy dog eyes behind it. "For me, Gracie. Please."

Grace frowned and huffed in displeasure. Lou knew she had her right where she wanted. "You know I'm powerless to deny you when you look at me like that. It isn't fair."

Lou brightened. "Does that mean you're going to put today behind you?"

"He treated me like I was a nobody," Grace whispered, withdrawing her hands from Lou's and crossing her arms. She looked out the window at the rapidly darkening sky.

As much as she hated to admit it, Anton's dismissive behavior had called up deeply buried feelings of worthlessness.

She blinked back tears quickly and took another deep drink of her wine. It stunk too much of home, of a place and time where her shortcomings had been pointed out at every turn. Grace had left that all behind when she'd taken her internship with Lou.

Hadn't she?

Maybe. Maybe not.

And her run-in with Anton told her more than likely the answer was a big fat hell-to-the-no.

She cleared her throat. "I'm pretty sure he talks to Siri with more manners than he talked to me, okay?" She shook her head and sighed, fingers tightening on the stem of her wine glass. "It wasn't that he thought I was a delivery girl. It's not what he called me; it's *how* he said it."

"I know, and it was out of line. I laid into him about it," Lou told her, prompting a surprised look.

"Really?"

"Of course. No one talks to my best friend like that and lives to tell the tale unscathed. He swears he didn't know it was you, but even if it had been a stranger it wasn't okay. He knows that and he wants to make it up to you."

"That won't be necessary." Grace toyed with her wineglass again. She was pleased at Lou's defense and smiled in spite of her anger at Anton. Who cared if she had nursed a tiny—okay massive—crush on the man?

He wasn't Lou. And Grace's heart beat for Lou.

The tiny scientist's loyalty was unwavering and it was

one of the major reasons Grace was determined to face down aliens at Lou's side. It was the least she could do for the woman who had never let her down. If they got abducted by extraterrestrials, then by god it was going to be together.

Grace's smile widened at the thought and Lou rolled her eyes.

"You're thinking about how we're going to get abducted by aliens together again, aren't you?"

Grace shrugged and looked down at her nails. "Look, all I'm saying is it's statistically plausible."

Lou raised her wine glass. "To our eventual unsolved disappearance."

Grace grinned. "But at least we'll be together."

They clinked glasses and settled back into their seats, but Grace raised an eyebrow when she noticed Lou studying her over the rim of her glass.

"What's with the sly look?"

It wasn't good when Lou got a sly look. The last time Lou had gotten a sly look they'd been arrested.

"You like him," Lou said.

"Like hell I do." Grace tossed her hair over her shoulder with a flick of her hand. "I don't have an opinion on him," she lied. She glanced away when she saw Lou raising an eyebrow. She knew she was lying, but that didn't mean she wanted her best friend pointing it out.

"So me telling you that he just walked in and is on his way over here is fine?" Lou asked, nodding over Grace's shoulder at the door.

"What? Where?" Grace's eyes widened in shock and she whirled around in her chair in the direction Lou had indicated, but she went still when a second later Lou's laughter rang in her ears.

"Gotcha!"

Grace closed her eyes and breathed. "You're such a brat," she hissed at her friend, turning around to see Lou giggling into her wine glass.

"You said you didn't have an opinion." Lou shrugged and looked down into her wine glass. "But that reaction has me thinking otherwise."

"I hate you sometimes."

"Yeah, I know. But let's get down to the real matter at hand." Lou looked up at her friend with a bright smile. "You are into Anton."

Grace pressed her fingers to her temples with another deep breath. "You're mad, woman. Too many hours staring at space has addled your brain."

"That may be, but that doesn't change the fact that I'm right."

Grace frowned and managed to meet the unwavering gaze of her friend for a whole three seconds before she groaned and threw up her hands. "Okay, so he's attractive, and I just so happened to notice after months of correspondence. Sue me!"

"I knew it," Lou crowed with a slap of her hand against the table. A pair of nearby diners gave them looks, but Grace gave them an apologetic shrug while Lou paid them no attention. "I knew it the second I saw the two of you fighting. What was in those emails? Why do you think I brought the spray bottle out?"

"About that." Grace held up a finger. "Why?"

"My grandma uses them on the cats when one goes

into heat," Lou told her matter-of-factly. "Given the sexual tension, I think I made the right call."

"You're not going to let this go, are you?"

Lou drew a line in the air with her hands. "Nope. Nein. Nyet."

"But I already promised to play nice."

Lou wiggled her eyebrows. "And I bet you're going to play reeeeal nice."

Grace groaned. "Never do that again."

"It's okay to be attracted to Anton."

"No, it's really not, Lou."

"And why not?"

"Because he *knows* he's hot, and besides, everyone knows about Anton Kovalev." Grace looked away, not wanting to say more because despite the wealth of public knowledge detailing exactly what kind of man Anton was she'd still fallen head over ass for the idiot.

"He's not like that anymore, you know? That was years ago."

"A leopard can't change its spots." His treatment of her had been proof enough that Anton Kovalev was still the spoiled brat the media had followed for years.

"Pish." Lou waved a hand. "I'm just telling you that Anton isn't who the media has made him out to be, and you should let him show you that."

"Are you sure? Because so far it seems like the media is spot-on about who Anton is." Grace leaned forward on her elbows and raised an eyebrow at her friend, who rolled her eyes in response. It was easy for Lou to dismiss her, she knew, but that was because her friend didn't know just how much Grace had fallen for the man.

She bit her lip and looked away, not willing to spill the beans on her stupid crush. She'd tell Lou at a different time.

A better time.

Like never.

"Give him a chance. He's not that playboy party monster they say he is. I mean, he was practically a kid when all that happened anyways."

"Twenty-four isn't a kid. I'm twenty-four right now."

"Well, just—" Lou opened and closed her mouth a couple times before she sighed and said, "Girls mature faster than boys?"

Grace's mouth dropped open. "You did not just—"

Lou winced. "It's the best argument I have at the moment, so I did. What I'm trying to say is Anton has done a lot of maturing over the last few years, and he's trying to make a difference in the world."

"You forgot womanizer, not just a party monster playboy," Grace said, as if Lou hadn't spoken, and sipped her wine with a smile when her friend grunted in frustration.

"So I did, but when's the last time you saw him in the papers about that? The man is practically a celibate monk now."

"Yeah, uh huh."

She drummed her fingers on the table. "I don't know why you're pressing the issue. You know I have abysmal taste in men."

"Except that Anton is a good man, which is exactly why I'm pushing the issue. This is proof."

"I don't know about this 'good man' business."

Lou held up a hand. "He is. I've known him for a good amount of time, and he is."

"Yes, bu—"

"Would it help if I told you why he was awful today?"

Grace bit her lip and then nodded. "Yes, actually, so lay it on me, boss lady."

"Anton's been working on some pretty revolutionary stuff. I'm talking obsessive work hours for at least a couple of years, and all of that work was stolen yesterday."

Grace's mouth dropped open. "What?"

That could only mean one thing: that RED had been stolen.

She felt her palms start to sweat at the idea. Anton had spent so much time on the infrared tech, telling her about developments over the past few months, waxing poetic until she started humming the wedding march whenever it came up in conversation.

RED meant the world—no, the universe—to Anton.

"That's why he's here. I invited him to get out of the media storm in New York. I got approval to add him and his team to ours. CERN was frothing at the mouth over the chance to have him here, so it wasn't a hard sell. But Anton wasn't in the best headspace when you two collided for the first time."

Grace looked down at the table with a frown. Still trying to process what Lou had disclosed about RED, she cleared her throat. "That much was apparent."

"Does what I told you change anything?"

She gave a quiet sigh before she said, "Yes."

"Good."

"What's he going to do about RED?"

Lou shrugged. "I don't know yet. The plan is for him to lay low here and get his head on straight while he helps me finish Beta's retrofitting."

"Betsy," Grace corrected without missing a beat. "Fine. I accept his presence with stoic indifference, but don't expect me to be buddy-buddy with him, okay? I understand that he was under a lot of pressure, but I'm not going to just act like our first face-to-face trainwreck didn't happen."

"Does not pretending it didn't happen encompass you being civil and professional?"

Grace tilted her head in consideration before she nodded. "It does."

An ill-fated crush on Anton didn't mean she couldn't do her job. She could do anything, was willing to do anything, for Lou, and treating Anton professionally was the least of these things.

"Then I'm fine with you holding a grudge."

"Who said I was going to hold a grudge?"

Lou snorted. "I know you."

Grace laughed. "Touché."

"COFFEE?"

Anton's head snapped up at the soft voice. He swallowed hard when he saw Grace holding a coffee cup out to him. He opened his mouth to say something, anything, but the way her eyes slid away from his shut him up.

"Black, right?" she asked, making him want to melt into the floor and evaporate into the atmosphere. She'd remembered his barked order from the day before, and all he could do was nod as he took the cup from her.

"Thank you," he murmured. Grace inclined her head, and then she turned away, already moving on to the next scientist with a smile and another cup of coffee.

Anton's lips pursed at the sight of her toothy grin, radiant and warm. It was a look Anton wished she had directed at him, and he stifled a sigh as he nursed his cup of coffee.

It was torture trying to sort out his own team and not be hyperaware of Grace as she flitted through the lab. Her mass of pink hair acted like a beacon, and he bit his lip at the sight of her thick hair all done in curls and pinned up in a perfect pairing to her red lipstick, rounding out the picture of a pinup from Anton's fantasies.

It was going to be a long day with Grace in the labs, and he wondered if he could cut his stint in Geneva short.

But what would he say?

That he had to beg off because he was inexplicably and distractedly attracted to the smart-mouthed lab assistant? That wouldn't be professional.

This was hardly how he envisioned spending his time recovering from RED's loss, but he supposed there were worse ways to go than distracted-to-death-by-pink-haired-goddesses.

"Anton, are you there?"

Mindy, his lab assistant, tapped her pen against his chest with a pinched look on her face as Anton stared off hopelessly at Grace, who laughed at whatever joke a tech had just told her.

Okay, so it was impossible for him not to pine. He

should be better than longing looks. He'd dated a princess, for heaven's sake! By god, he was debonair. When had he turned back into a pre-teen with a crush?

"Right, sorry, sorry." He ducked his head and forced his attention back to the inventory list Mindy had been going over with him. She raised an eyebrow but said nothing else, for which he was grateful.

The last thing he needed was for someone to comment on his behavior.

He wiggled his pen in his hand and glanced at Grace again. It was new to him to not be the focus of attention, and it puzzled him.

How did this work? Was he supposed to wait for her to approach him? Or were they forever doomed to dance around one another in the labs? Would he be able to bring up one of the books she loved and use that as a bridge back to whatever they had almost been?

He looked away from the list in his hands and smirked when he met Grace's stare. Instantly she looked away, but he didn't miss the pretty pink blush that dusted her cheeks. A second later she worried her bottom lip, dark eyes darting back up to meet his. Anton had to stifle a groan at the sight of the pastel-haired woman looking up at him through her lashes.

The effect was immediate, even from across the room, and he took an unconscious step toward her, but Mindy clearing her throat once more made him freeze in his tracks.

"Why don't you just go talk to her already?" Mindy sighed, giving him a solid whack with her clipboard.

"I have no idea what you're talking about," he said, feigning interest in the papers in front of him.

She rolled her eyes. "Sure you don't. Why don't you just sign off on these papers and you'll be free to ogle in peace? I'm pretty sure she'd even let you go over there and talk to her if you made the effort. Maybe say sorry for whatever you've done."

Anton grabbed the form she held and began to sign at random. "What makes you say that?" he asked, keeping his voice cool and eyes trained on the papers in front of him.

When Mindy didn't answer, Anton raised his eyes to see her grinning.

"Because she can't seem to stop looking at your ass every chance she gets. She's not as good at being covert as she thinks. I've counted her copping a look no less than fourteen times since this morning. Yes, I've been counting, and number fifteen is occurring as we speak. I thought you used to be a lady killer. Don't look at her!"

Anton lifted one shoulder. "This is more fun." He nearly pumped his fist in victory when he saw that the pink-haired beauty's eyes had fixed on his backside.

A nudge from a passing Lou prompted an audible squeak from Grace, who dropped out of sight behind the lab table she stood beside.

"Did she just stop, drop, and roll behind that table?" Minus said.

"Yup." He grinned. Now this he was familiar with. He rubbed his hands together.

"Go talk to her."

"Soon," Anton said, turning his back to where Grace

had dropped out of sight. He rolled his shoulders and studied the forms in front of him.

He may or may not have turned his back to her on purpose because, as the old adage went, *shake what yo mama gave ya.*

If she had been staring at his ass, then surely he had more to tempt her with, right?

CHAPTER THREE

"It's easier to ask forgiveness than it is to get permission."
—Grace Hopper

"You wanna tell me why you've been ogling Anton's ass all day?"

"Is he still looking?" Grace hissed. She sat on the floor, back pressed up against the lab table, hands covering her face.

"Yup."

"By Odin's beard," Grace cursed, letting her head bang back against the table. She hadn't meant to be caught mid-deed, but there was something to be said about a man who knew his measurements and how to display them. And that was exactly what the scientist had done, and on purpose, too.

There was no missing the fact that Anton's eyes were on her often, nor was she oblivious enough to not realize he'd caught her practically drooling over him. If not him, then at the very least his assistant was on to her. The other woman had caught her no less than a dozen times staring at Anton.

Grace had been set up, and they both knew it. The timing of his last glance at her had been too perfect to be coincidence, as had been the knowing smirk on his face. The jersey knit of Anton's sweats shouldn't have been showing her as much of his backside as it had, but here she was, shamefaced and in hiding.

He planned on torturing her. To what end she hadn't figured out yet. What could he possibly want from her?

Monday on a Friday, indeed.

"You planning on getting up from there sometime today, or should I just have everything sent to you here?" Lou asked, hitching a hip against the table.

Grace sighed. "Would that be too drastic of a career choice?"

"Just a smidge." Lou pinched her fingers together in illustration and then held her hand out to Grace. "Get back up here. It's just a butt."

"Easy for you to say," Grace grumbled, taking her friend's hand and standing up. She kept her eyes averted from the side of the lab where Anton's team milled about, which amounted to her being unable to turn her neck further than fifteen degrees to the left and certainly didn't account for a route to the bathroom or out of the lab.

She rubbed her temples. This was not going well.

"It's easy for me to say because I've learned how to be covert."

"You've been looking too? I knew it." Grace laughed, grateful for the distraction.

"Keep it down. Don't bring the rest of us down with you."

"What happened to 'it's just a butt'?"

"It's just a butt when *you're* caught looking, but I'm the boss. I can't be caught. I've still got a project to see through with him, you know."

Grace rolled her eyes and executed a less-than-nimble turn to the right. "Can I please make this day a little better and get the s'mores and stars party all prepped?"

"Grace...there's so much to do. We have that brand new pulsar timing array that I need to get cracking on. You know it's going to take us weeks to get it sorted. I'm pretty sure we have a bunch of young pulsars from glancing through the data."

"But party…"

"It took us weeks to get these readings. Three weeks, to be exact," she said, holding up three fingers and making Grace roll her eyes.

"And that's why one more night isn't going to kill us. Besides, it's tomorrow so you can use the rest of today to ogle your science," Grace said with what was definitely not a pout, because lab queens did not pout when their science bosses couldn't see reason enough to relax. "Just one night is all I'm asking for, and then we can go wild with back to business as usual with all the glitches and possible black hole collisions."

"Oh, is that right?"

Grace nodded, sensing her friend weakening under the promise of data readings. "So many pulsar waves. More than you can shake a stick at. I bet you we find at least two new black holes."

Lou tapped her chin for a second and let out a hum as she feigned deep thought, but a second later a warm smile lit her face. "Yes. Permission granted."

"Perfect, because I already have the permit too. Here it is!" Grace slapped the pink paper she'd picked up earlier that week from the good people of Telepherique du Salève for the overnight use of both the steam-powered tram to the top of Mont Salève and a cozy little spot for a bonfire replete with a fantastic view of Jura and Mont Blanc. It was the stuff of European daydreams, and Grace was ready to say just as much when Lou huffed a sigh.

"What if I had said no?" Lou crossed her arms.

"You wouldn't." Grace shrugged and gave her friend an excited squeeze. "This is the thing we used to talk about while we were in exile in Arizona. Besides, you can't return liquor, and I already bought it *and* burned the receipts, so no takesies backsies! We're going to have a sweet little bonfire with a wonderful chance to stargaze, and everyone is going to be happy. I just have to get it all up there."

"You know I don't do well with the outdoors." Lou shuddered and wrapped her arms around herself with a pained look. "Nature is an absolute war zone for me. When you mentioned a party, I thought it would be at a bar in town."

Grace rolled her eyes, already pocketing the permit. "Bars are boring. This is next-level Geneva living, lady. We have the bonfire all prepped and ready to go and a genuine steam-powered cable car to cart us up like royalty, with insane night views. I'm bringing booze and s'mores fixings, so don't scowl at me. You love s'mores.

Plus, there's a restaurant nearby, just in case you feel the need to mutiny."

Lou perked up. "What kind of restaurant?"

"The fancy French kind, so what else do we need? And it used to be an observatory during WWI, and that means I thought about everything. Wholesome fun for the whole science family."

"Are you inviting Anton and his team, too?"

Grace swallowed hard past the embarrassment caused by her inability to creep in peace, but she blew out a resigned sigh. "Of course I am."

"Perfect! Then let's do it."

"Yippee," Grace muttered, her mood dampened by the prospect of facing Anton and his butt. It was going to be a trying night. She was going to have to do better if she hoped to survive the night in one piece.

"Oh, now who's pouting?" Lou bumped her hip against Grace's and winked. "If you invite them you can stare at his butt under the cover of darkness."

"I don't pout. Lab queens do not pout," Grace muttered and turned away from Lou with a flourish, her hands already snatching up her bag. If she was going to invite Anton and his band of astrophysicists, then she was going to need more supplies, particularly of the alcohol and chocolate variety.

"I swear, you get caught staring at one damn butt and you never live it down," she sighed, but there was a smile on her face that had Lou laughing and Anton staring after her from agar.

~

It was a universally acknowledged truth that any scientist in possession of a massive brain and ambitious designs on unlocking the universe's secrets was in need of an excuse to relax, and Grace's stargazing and s'mores shindig was just the occasion to provide such relief.

She had procured the booze, an assortment of bubbly champagne, wines, liquors dark to light, and every manner of beer from hops to stout, and had managed to acquire the must-have ingredients of graham crackers, marshmallows, and chocolate bars known the world over for comprising the all mighty s'more.

The only thing standing in the way of Grace throwing a fun-filled night for her team—well, and Anton's team—was one simple matter: how in the wild blue yonder was she going to transport what looked like a metric ton of supplies to her chosen party site?

She tapped her chin and walked around the pallets, which had just been dropped off in front of the shipping and receiving dock. When she ordered everything she apparently hadn't quite thought through the finer details of moving her party loot from point A to point B.

Or rather, when she had made the plans she hadn't realized that Anton's arrival in Geneva would coincide so that all available manpower capable of lifting anything more than a pipette would be otherwise assigned.

She pursed her lips and glanced over her shoulder at the flurry of activity going on all around her. Her eyes slid to the side as she took in the army of workers focused on unloading Anton's equipment. The man had brought enough to start his own lab.

Her nose wrinkled and she bit back the thought that

she wished he would start his own lab somewhere far away and very much out of sight. Preferably a place where their paths would never, ever cross—except for the inevitable demise of the planet due to a cosmological event in which they'd all be called together to save the world—but given their first meeting, even that might be too soon.

"Of course he has everyone working for him," she muttered, hands going to her hips.

This was going to require more thought...more sweet talking. What should have been a happy event, one she had spent far too many hours daydreaming about, had crashed and burned before she had even had the opportunity to introduce herself, and now he had the audacity to hog all the beefy muscle in the region to move in.

"Asshole," she sighed, looking down at the tablet she clutched. How many times had she opened an email from him with embarrassing eagerness, or stopped to save an article she knew he'd enjoy? Now all she wanted to see from him was a departure notice.

Except, with the bustle of the warehouse there was no indication that Anton intended for his stay to be brief. If the forklifts and men with impressive biceps unloading crates were anything to go by, this was going to be for the long haul.

She had done harder things than endure the presence of one spoiled, egotistical, smart-mouthed scientist. She could do it—*would* do it for the sake of Lou's research and the success of Betsy. And what better way to kick off her study in patience and professionalism than a party?

She wouldn't give Anton another thought, unless it

was related to work or otherwise avoiding him at any time and point not required by work.

Speaking of which, she needed to make like a banana and split before she ran into said astrophysicist. There was no way the man would be able to stay away while others handled his tech. She was surely lucky they hadn't crossed paths yet.

Grace glanced back over at the busy loading dock and let out a hum of consideration. She could move the load of sweets and drinks at her back, but it would take some time...unless she managed to lure away one or five of the workers. Or the heavy machinery they operated. Hey, as long as she got them back in a timely fashion and got them to swear a vow of secrecy, right?

There was no real harm in that.

They'd be back before Anton knew, and secrets made super friends. She could always use more friends, and she was sure the denizens of the loading docks would make for wonderful additions to her friend circle. The more the merrier, especially when those friends came with muscles as big as her head and forklift know-how.

Grace straightened her shoulders and sucked in a deep breath. She could do this, if she said the right combination of platitudes and promises of s'mores. Who wasn't willing to work for treats?

She had just set off for the first candidate for new best friend-slash-heavy machinery operator when Anton stepped around a corner of graham crackers with a raised eyebrow. He glanced at the tower of carbohydrates and gave it an assessing look before he nodded at her.

"Hey," he said, as if they were still friends.

Her heart clenched at the familiar way his voice slid over her, at the warm feelings that made her want to step toward him.

That was over. Cancelled.

The man she had felt that for, had crushed on for months, wasn't real. He couldn't be, if yesterday was anything to go by.

"What do you want?" she asked, hugging her tablet close to her chest.

"Is that how they say hi in Geneva?" Anton asked, leaning against the tower of graham crackers and crossing his arms.

She shrugged, looking at her tablet, which had nothing open at the moment besides a doodle app she'd just downloaded. "I wouldn't know. I don't leave the labs," she replied in a tone that was all business, and made a show of swiping across the tablet to paint little smiley faces here and there.

"You leave plenty. You were telling me about that hike and your big night out last time we talked."

Her finger jerked across the tablet screen, a misplaced line appearing across her picture. She took a step back and raised her eyes to glare at him. "What do you know about my big night out?"

"I know you had too many G&Ts that night."

"Lucky guess," she shot back. "Anyone and everyone does that. Why are you even talking to me?"

"I know you called me after."

"So what? You emailed me and I...was being proficient by returning your call with the time difference."

"Pretty sure work wasn't on your mind when you

called me, Grace."

Her heart started pounding at the memory of how much she had enjoyed hearing his voice. How much it had pained her not to call him after that, because that call had been on the borderline of something...something bigger and hotter and definitely not work appropriate.

Thank Odin she'd had the self-restraint to not call him after that. Where would she be now, after their first face-to-face meeting?

Devastated, that was where.

"That's supposition," she huffed, looking back down at her tablet and scribbling some spaghetti hair on a smiley face.

He rubbed a hand along his jaw and fixed her with a soulful look he had no right wielding. She was certain it had been calibrated to weaken a woman's strength of will. Or at least she guessed it was, because she decided to offer the most grown-up response to Anton's unwavering attention: she refused to look at him.

"That's generally what you do when you see a friend," he told her.

"We aren't friends," she said, redoubling her efforts to avoid his gaze.

"Grace…"

"What? We are not friends. We were, but—"

"But what?" he asked, closing the distance between them with shocking speed. She looked up at him to see a pained look on his face.

She matched his movement by backing up, and bumped into a case of beer with an "oof". He reached out a hand to steady her.

"But nothing," she insisted, righting herself and jumping away from his outstretched hand. "We are not friends. Period. End of story."

"It doesn't have to be that way. We were friends. We *are* friends, Grace."

She shook her head so hard her hair whipped into her face. "Friends don't talk to each other the way you did to me yesterday."

He pinched the bridge of his nose and groaned. "Grace, look, that wasn't the best way to meet, but I didn't know it was you."

"That's not the point, Anton. I don't care if you knew it was me or not—you don't treat people like that. You were insufferable." She punctuated the last word with another tap of her finger to the tablet, which added a kitten sticker to the crude technicolor drawing.

"I know I was, but things were tense with me coming to Geneva."

Her mouth twisted in a frown. "Why? Because you lost your tech? That doesn't give you the right to talk to people the way you did to me. Besides, don't think I didn't smell the booze on you."

He winced. "Grace—"

"And now here you are, acting like nothing happened and I should just—what? Pretend nothing happened, too?"

His facial expression morphed into downright shocked, and she found that she didn't much care for it.

In fact, it ticked her off so badly she swore she saw double for a hot second before she was able to use the solid wall of graham crackers at her side to ground herself.

"Grace, listen," Anton tried again, but the slap of Grace's free hand against the box of graham crackers cut him off.

"No, you listen, Anton," she said, punctuating her words with a tap of her fingers against the graham cracker boxes, and whirled around to face him. "You were my friend."

"Grace—"

This time it was she who marched forward, backing him up, gesturing with her tablet. "For months we talked and got to know each other, and you don't know how much those messages meant to me. How much hearing from you meant to me."

His brows knit together in concern. "Those messages meant something to me too."

"Then why did you—" She stopped speaking when her voice cracked, and she looked away from him. "It doesn't matter why you did what you did. You hurt me."

"I didn't mean to. You have to believe that. It was a mistake."

When he made to shift toward her, Grace snatched up a five pound bag of marshmallows, a risky move given that she still waved her tablet in the other hand, and pretended to give the marshmallows an assessing look.

"Mistake or not, it happened, and there's no going back."

"Why not?" Anton asked, voice soft. "Why isn't there? We can be friends again. It was one day. We've had so many other days and conversations, Grace."

Her hand tightened on the bag of marshmallows and she forced a thin smile. "Because out of all of those days, that one, Anton, mattered the most." She blinked against the telltale stinging of her eyes that meant she was close to tears. She would have given her right arm for the ability to adopt an unaffected air in this moment.

Why couldn't she be frosty and perfunctory when confronted with him? Why was she nearly in tears and clutching marshmallow as if her life depended on it?

"Do you know how much I—" Her throat closed around the lump in it, moving her a little closer to the threshold of tears than she was comfortable with, so she did what any self-respecting woman waving a bag of marshmallow fluff and a tablet with a stick figure drawing could do when she hoped to save face. "I have a lot of work to do, Anton. I'll—well, if you have anything I need to take care of, have Mindy send it my way, please."

His face darkened and his shoulders drooped. "Work isn't what's important here, Grace. We need to talk about what happened."

She shifted the marshmallow bag, which she'd squeezed into a single malformed lump of playdoh, to the top of the tablet and gave both a shake. "What happened?" she asked, eliciting a nod from Anton. "Okay, here's what happened. You hurt me, but it's okay. I'm a big girl, and that means I conveniently own a pair of big girl panties I can put on, which means we will work together just fine. Now, if you'll excuse me." She held up the tablet and marshmallow bag duo and gave them a little shake. "I have to move all of this on my own."

"Where are you moving it?" he asked.

"Nunya," she replied, glaring at the mountain of treats in front of her.

When she had ordered it all, the plan had seemed simple: purchase copious amounts of alcohol and enough supplies for s'mores to drown a boy scout troop, and use said supplies to throw a s'mores party that would be talked about forever.

What Grace hadn't really considered in her party supply buying frenzy was transporting her goods to the top of Mont Salève. To be fair, she had counted on the usual manpower normally roaming the docks in bountiful supply. All a lady needed on those days was a please and a thank you.

She scowled at the crew moving Anton's tech. She'd be lucky if she could pry a dolly from them at this point.

"Real mature," he replied, crossing his arms.

She stuck out her tongue. "It wasn't intended to be. Now if you'll excuse me, I have to get a move on, and I don't particularly feel like talking to you because, big girl panties or not, I'm still mad at you."

"Where are you moving all of this stuff to?" Anton asked again, ignoring her glare, which Grace might have been impressed at under normal circumstances, but all it did was feed her annoyance at the man.

"Mont Salève," she bit out, narrowing her eyes and trying to increase the heat of her stare by a good thirty degrees celsius.

He sighed, tipping his chin down, and gave her a dispassionate look. "You trying to stare me down might be impressive if I hadn't spent most of my school days under the care of Europe's most severe instructors. You'll have to try harder, Grace."

"Damn boarding school kids. You're supposed to be as

soft as the marshmallow puff in my hands." She shook the bag for emphasis.

"A true menace." Grace scowled again, which only made him grin at her. "How are you going to get all of this up there? You have to go by tram."

She gritted her teeth and strangled the marshmallows within an inch of their sugary lives. "I know. When I fever-dreamed up the whole thing I didn't realize just how involved your move would be."

Anton hummed when he saw the narrow-eyed glare she shot toward the army of workers unloading his gear from New York. "You need help," he said, voice even.

"Maybe," she replied, not meeting his eyes, and threw the marshmallow lump off her tablet and back into the heap of other marshmallow bags.

He gestured at the supplies with a raised eyebrow. "How are you going to move all of this?"

"With my two hands."

"That's it? You're going to need more than that, Grace."

"Then it's a good thing I have a pair of legs too," she shot back, pointing down with a flick of her finger.

He rolled his eyes and crossed his arms. "Grace, take some of the guys helping me."

"I'll be okay." She turned her back on him and made a show of checking things off on her tablet. Now her drawing had a nice pair of trees and a smiling sun. If she kept this up she'd have a regular Renaissance painting by the end of their conversation. "Really. I've got it," she added when he stepped closer, but he wasn't in the mood to let her brush him off.

"Grace, take the help. There's plenty of manpower

here and not all of them need to be working on getting me unloaded. I don't care if you have two legs and arms. You're going to need at least four times that to make a dent in moving this stuff."

She jutted her chin. "I'm fine."

"I'll have them come over and get to work," he said with a sigh when she showed no sign of budging on the matter.

She whirled around to face him with a glare. "I can do it. I don't need your help."

"You do, but you're just mad at me, and you shouldn't let that make things harder for yourself. I don't know what all of this is for, but why are you going to kill yourself doing extra work? We both know you already work hard enough without this on top of it. You're going to run yourself into the ground, and for what? A little pride? It's not worth it, Grace. I'll have some guys over here and whatever else you need to get everything set up, okay?"

He wasn't wrong that her team needed it or that she was already burning the candle at both ends. It was chaotic around her labs, but she thrived in it for the simple reason that it involved taking care of those she considered family.

She shouldn't like that he knew that about her.

It wasn't smart.

She looked down at her feet and almost groaned at herself. She'd never been good at making great decisions.

"Yeah, fine, okay."

"Good."

"Thank you," she managed to get out before he

rounded the graham crackers. He stopped there and glanced back at her, a rueful smile on his face.

"Of course."

And then he was gone, and she was left clutching her tablet to her chest. She sighed and grabbed a chocolate bar from its box with a groan before she ripped it open and took a healthy bite.

Chocolate was always there. Chocolate understood. And if she had a prayer of making it through the party she most certainly needed to inhale the chocolate bar she had begun to eat.

She paused and gave the s'mores horde another considering look. If she was going to survive close quarters with Anton and his team, then no one could fault her for keeping a few bars for herself, now could they?

After she had weighed herself down with candy bars, she let out a satisfied hum and patted the bulk in her pockets with a smile.

She could do this.

Her candy loot said so.

CHAPTER FOUR

"Physics is, hopefully, simple. Physicists are not."
—Edward Teller

Anton stretched with a grimace and stood from his seat. It had been a long day, one that had drowned him with paperwork.

He hated paperwork.

If he never saw another triplicate form again it would be too soon, but regrettably there were things he couldn't get out of, no matter how many stamps of his signature he made and gifted to Mindy. She wouldn't have it, not after the Picasso incident.

But at least now he owned a Picasso, which was always a positive.

"Where do you think you're going?" Mindy appeared at his side, her eyes on the forms she had left in front of him.

"Out. Away from here, you taskmaster. I signed every

last one of these." Anton held up a hand to stop her when she raised a skeptical eyebrow. "I verified and reviewed each and every last line item, so don't think I didn't notice you included a fifteen-page inventory list detailing the dinosaurs of Jurassic Park."

Mindy gave him an appraising look. "I'm impressed."

"Then my job is done. Now, which way to the closest bar? I need a drink after all of that."

He shrugged on his coat, already thinking of what he wanted for dinner, when Mindy said, "No bar tonight."

"Why the hell not? I did my time today. I deserve yard time for good behavior," Anton whined. He knew it wasn't dignified, but it was what it was—a whine he felt entitled to, after the torture he had endured over the last three hours, and without the slightest glimpse of Grace's pink curls.

The woman had disappeared hours before with a grin on her face that made Anton feel like he was stuck in a dryer on the spin cycle. That, or eating a ghost pepper. One or the other.

"Because we're going to a stargazing and s'mores shindig."

Anton took the flyer she handed him to see an arrangement of clip art's finest, featuring said s'mores and stargazing. At the top was a bonfire in black sharpie with a stick figure beside it yelling, *WOW! YOU'RE INVITED! SO COOL!*

"What is this?"

"Team-building exercise," Mindy said, scooping up the papers he had signed. "The cutie ogling you is putting it together, and we're all invited. We're leaving in twenty."

"But—"

"See you then," Mindy said, turning toward the lab door, but she hesitated and glanced over her shoulder at him. "Or else, Anton."

"Fine." Anton waved the flyer in surrender and, appeased, Mindy set off again. He watched her until she rounded the corner before looking back down at the flyer in his hand, and he chuckled.

"So that's what she was up to," he mused, thinking back on her refusal to tell him why she needed to move the inexplicable mixture of alcohol and sweets to the top of Mont Salève. Anton had been dismayed at her absence from the labs, but at the prospect of spending the night with her—and if the clip art was any indication, in the company of both s'mores and booze—he grew more optimistic.

This was where he could turn on the Kovalev charm. Where he could capitalize on catching Grace in the act of...admiring him, but what would that entail?

Sweet-talk her under the stars, catch her eye across the bonfire, or maybe something as simple as a smile with the right kind of heat to bring her to him?

"Where who went?" a voice asked, causing Anton to jump approximately four feet off the ground.

"Holy hell," he wheezed and whirled around to see Lou regarding him with a curious look. Anton sagged against the table and shook his head. "Wear a bell or something to warn a man, will you?! You almost sent me into cardiac arrest."

"Small and sudden doses of adrenaline increase antioxidants, so you're welcome," she said, sauntering toward him. "Where who went?" she repeated, which only made Anton grit his teeth.

He could already tell from the sly look in Lou's eyes that she knew exactly who he meant.

"I'm not going to dignify that question with an answer."

"So haughty." She crossed her arms and smiled at him. "Are you going to actually talk to her, or are you just going to keep staring at each other when you think the other one isn't looking?"

"I have no idea what you're talking about."

"You're a terrible liar."

"Not true. I was, at one time, a shameless degenerate. A regular lothario, if you will. I am quite skilled at bending the truth."

Lou snorted. "Yeah, yeah, but we both know that isn't really you, so answer me this. When are you going to talk to Gracie? And also, for how long have you two been talking, eh?"

Anton rolled his eyes heavenward. What had he done to deserve such meddlesome people in his life? He was a good person, wasn't he?

After all the damage he'd wrought as a young twenty-something, Anton had made sure to give his time and money where it was needed most. He'd created mentoring and scholarship programs focused on economically disadvantaged students, and financially and publicly backed initiatives aimed at increasing diversity in the world of science, because who really wanted to listen to the same five old white men prattle on?

That had to count for something, didn't it?

It seemed it didn't.

She cleared her throat, interrupting his internal crisis, and he sighed. "Tonight. At the shindig." He paused and held up a hand. "What do you mean, for how long have we been talking? She's been the go-between for us for the past six months."

"That's not the talking I'm referring to and you know it. She's my best friend. You think I can't tell when something is going on?" Anton spluttered and Lou pushed on, ignoring his reaction. "Now, your version of sorry doesn't include you trying to seduce her, right?"

He stiffened and when he said nothing, she groaned and shook a finger at him.

"But I can be very charming and—"

"*N* to the *O*." Lou shook her head. "That notorious playboy schtick isn't going to work on Grace. You're going to have to do better."

"Schtick? It isn't stand-up comedy, Lou."

"May as well be."

"Brutal."

"I prefer honest."

"Fine, since you're the Grace Whisperer, what do you suggest I do? You want me to talk to her, right? What's the best tactic when I do?"

"First of all, don't use a tactic." She gave him a pinched look. "She's going to see right through it, and you'll be out on your good-looking ass."

Anton's cheeks colored but he straightened his shoulders. "Women like looking at me. That's what I'm leading with."

"It's not a bad start. She does like looking at you."

He smirked. "I noticed."

"But before you go around trying to seduce her, you need to know that Grace is going to need...a little more out of you."

Anton steepled his fingers and regarded her over them. "So no one-night stands?"

Lou gave him a withering look. "No."

"Well, shit."

"Do not tell me that was your plan."

Anton made a show of not meeting the small physicist's eyes. "Who can say? My memory is terrible these days."

"I swear to—" She stood up abruptly and whacked him on the arm. "No one-night stands."

"Why not? I think she'd quite like it. I know I would."

Lou's small hands shot out and grabbed Anton by his coat lapels and jerked him down until he was eye-to-eye with her. "I love you. I respect you. But if you think you're going to take advantage of my best friend I'll maim you and make it look like an accident." She paused and then added, "But not before I get your suggestions for how to retrofit the telescope."

"Just keeping me around for my wares then, I see."

Lou shrugged and gave him a shake. "Tale as old as time. Now, like I said, I'll maim you once we get the new infrared lens rig in then...."

Anton's eyes widened at the threat. "Wow, Lou. That's dark."

"Just say you're sorry."

"I—what?" He blinked, trying to keep up with the sudden shift in direction from Lou's threat, and cleared his throat. "Sorry, I'm still back where you were threatening me."

"Promises aren't threats, Anton." Lou let him go and he felt a shiver go down his spine at the sure look in Lou's eyes. He made a mental note: never cross Lou Wright. Ever. Not even on pain of death.

"You're scary."

The tiny woman shrugged. "Say you're sorry. It's that simple."

"To Grace?" Anton ventured, taking a small step back now that he was free from Lou's grip.

"She doesn't need fancy words, just real ones, Anton. If you say you're sorry and mean it, then all will be forgiven and you'll get bagels with your coffee. She'll even let you take her on a date. A sincere apology is all it'll take."

Anton squirmed at the remarkably simple suggestion. He wouldn't need flowery language or the right mood lighting to win Grace over. It was that easy, that honest, and he frowned at not having thought of it himself.

An apology had been the furthest thing from his mind when the party invitation had been announced. Anton wasn't sure he liked what that said about him, or how he lived his life.

He pushed the troubling thoughts away. This was not the time or the place for soul-searching, so he pasted a thousand-watt smile worthy of the paparazzi on his face and nodded at Lou, all pretense of his unsettled thoughts gone.

"I like bagels."

"That's not the only thing you like."

Anton's cheeks flushed. "She's smart and funny, so sue me."

"It's beautiful." Lou leaned closer, her palms on the glass of the tram car they rode to the top of Mont Salève. The cable car swayed as it moved up the mountainside, a full view of Geneva sprawling beneath them, creating a breathtaking sight.

"It's magical," Grace added, coming to stand beside her friend. The tram car was full of science minions, and while they were normally a chattering and bustling group, the scenic view was enough to render them silent, if only for the short duration of the ride. Grace turned, smiling at seeing the scientists all staring out into the night. They seemed contemplative and even calm, which was what she had hoped for. It was no easy feat to relax so many high-strung smarty pantses wound tighter than a two-dollar watch.

She looked out the window behind Lou to the tram car behind theirs. It was packed full of Anton and his own science tribe. She felt her cheeks warm with a blush when her eyes sought out Anton's figure.

He looked...good. Real good, in his dark peacoat and tousled hair.

Christ. Why did he have to be so attractive?

Grace turned away with a frown. She had been doing her duty as Lab Queen, albeit a Lab Queen obeying orders from her best friend to be polite and professional, both of which she found to be bittersweet. Yes, it was so very nice and wonderful to grow as an adult, but why did it have to come at the expense of experiencing immediate satisfaction?

The cable car came to its summit and slowed to a stop. The change in trajectory snapped Grace out of her musings, and she leapt into action. She had booze to peddle and s'mores to cook for her science brood, lest they rise up in mutiny. Already there were grumblings about "being forced into the wilds," and Grace was sure she'd heard Lou utter an oath at nature when the tram doors parted with a whoosh. Grace leaped out of the tram with a wave of her arms.

"Follow me to mystery and mayhem!" she called. She did her best to keep her voice excited, but when she twirled around to beckon them forward she saw a quiet group of science minions shuffling off the tram. She bit her lip at the sight.

They looked more like extras from a zombie television show than would-be revelers.

What had happened to their awe at the gorgeous views? Maybe an outdoor activity had been the wrong track with them after all…

Grace had just turned a beseeching look on Lou to rally the troops, but the second tram's arrival interrupted her.

"Did I hear mayhem?" Anton asked, stepping off the cable car with all the pomp of a prince, a bottle of Moët and Chandon in one hand. "Because you can't just bandy that word about without intent. It isn't civilized."

"There's mayhem, alright, especially with three dozen

agoraphobes dumped on a mountain top," Lou retorted, looking around herself.

Anton wrinkled his nose as he walked forward, fingers already moving to pop the cork from the bottle he held. "Sounds beastly when you put it that way. Like one of those reality television ordeals. Tell you what." He popped the cork with a flick of his wrist and gave Lou as charming a smile as Grace had ever seen. "Why don't I pour you a glass of this..." He held out a hand and Grace watched with disbelief as his assistant magicked a small plastic cup out of the ether. "And we'll see if that doesn't put some courage in your heart."

Lou eyed the glass. "I don't know. It may be for the best if I keep my wits about me, given my track record with nature."

"It would be irresponsible not to drink."

Lou arched an unconvinced eyebrow at him while the scientists at her back mirrored her skepticism at Anton's logic. "How so?"

"Already popped it. Absolutely cannot go to waste. That means it would be wasteful *and* irresponsible." He paused and gave Lou another winning smile before he shifted his gaze to Grace. "You can't have s'mores without booze. It's barbaric. Besides, Grace, ah, went through some effort to put this outing together. So drink." Anton began pouring out glasses for everyone as he spoke, and Grace dimly registered the faint popping sound of another bottle that his seemingly magical assistant had uncorked. "Get some fresh air, for god sake, it's good for you."

Grace watched Anton administer Moët to the troupe

of scientists, who were considerably more compliant with a glass of bubbly in hand. It was astonishing how fast the man had turned the night around.

He had saved the start of the party.

Grace stepped off to the side in shock at the realization, but she supposed she shouldn't have been surprised at how deftly he had handled the situation.

Getting a party off to a good start was old hat for a man like Anton.

"Grace?" Anton appeared suddenly at her side with a glass extended toward her. "Would you care for a drink?"

Her eyes fell to the glass in astonishment. First he had saved the party, and now...he was serving *her?* Had she fall into an alternate timeline?

Her heart ached in her chest.

This, *this* was her Anton. But for how long could she count on him staying?

"Oh, thank you." Grace took the cup with a weak smile. Anton gave her a quick nod, and she tried not to notice how he fell into step beside her as she walked toward the trail that would lead them to the bonfire.

"All right, you lushes!" She put a heavy dose of bravado into her voice as Anton kept walking close to her. They neared the path Grace had lined with fairy lights meant to keep her science tribe safe and sound from wandering off. How they could navigate the cosmos but lose all sense of self and direction the moment they set foot outside the lab she would never know. "Follow the pretty trail to s'mores and stars!"

"Will there be more of this?" An anonymous hand waved a glass of champagne.

"Yes! Bottles on bottles of it!" Grace answered, prompting a little cheer from the physicists clamoring up the trail on their merry way to the bonfire site.

Grace blew out a sigh, watching the pack of happy people, and she relaxed at the sight. Or she might have, if Anton hadn't entered her peripheral vision.

"Fickle bunch," he commented as they walked.

Grace tried not to notice how they had fallen behind the group, who in their excitement had pushed ahead at a surprising pace, leaving her alone with Anton.

"Well, you know how science minions are." The words slipped out before she could stop them, and she took a hasty sip from her cup when Anton laughed.

Odin.

The man had a sensational laugh.

She'd always thought so during their late night phone calls, but the effect in person? And she felt it even more so after he had rescued the evening.

Gratitude was a hell of a drug.

"Science minions?"

"Mmm." Grace swallowed down her glass in an impressive gulp. In her defense, the glass was tiny. She was *not* nervous.

Absolutely *not*.

Anton chuckled. "What does that make you if they are minions?"

"Their queen," Grace replied smoothly.

"Mm, a queen?" He stopped and gave her a considering look, a look that moved from her feet to her face, and Grace felt a blush heat her cheeks at the slow drag of Anton's eyes up her body.

Was he...checking her out?

Whatever it was, there was certainly no trace of the disdain in his eyes from the previous day.

She had daydreamed of him looking at her like that.

She gave a jerky nod, feeling emboldened by the champagne. "That's right."

"No one told me I was in the company of royalty. You'll have to excuse my manners, your majesty."

A giggle escaped Grace. She clapped a hand over her mouth in shock and took a quick step away from Anton, but the man was undeterred.

She should not be falling into their easy banter like this. It was too soon. Didn't she have any sense of self-preservation?

She couldn't trust him.

She leaned away from him, but Anton matched her step with one of his own and then dropped into a low bow, one that mirrored the bow he had given her on their first meeting...but this time it was different. For all of its silliness, the bow felt sincere. Anton raised his eyes to her as he straightened and nodded at her empty cup.

"May I?"

"What?" Grace blinked, still trying to process the new dynamic between Anton and herself. She had gone from wanting him to hating him, to lusting after him, and now to laughing with him. It was...a lot.

"A refresher? You seemed thirsty," Anton said, pointing at the bottle he held.

"Oh, yes, please." Grace held out her cup to him, grateful for something to do that didn't require her to meet his eyes. He had eyes too fine to be staring at on a pretty starry night, when one had been imbibing at top speed on a path lit up like something out of a romcom.

Dangerous territory. Down right perilous, even.

Anton poured her a fresh glass and the pair resumed walking, but this time the silence was nice, comfortable even. Grace had almost worked up the courage to ask after Anton's day when he spoke.

"I'm very sorry for my behavior."

"I—what?" Grace stopped in her tracks.

"Yesterday," Anton said, turning to face her and swallowing hard before he continued, "I was an absolute ass. You didn't deserve any of it. I am sorry."

"Oh," she sighed and looked down at her feet, unsure what to say. "Thank you." She paused then and added, "I forgive you."

Anton's face brightened. "Ah, I see you are a benevolent queen."

Grace nodded, smiling back. It was impossible not to when he beamed at her. His smile was downright infectious. How was this the man who had mistreated her?

"A good queen forgives, but I should apologize, too."

"Oh? How so?"

"Well," Grace said, and took a step down the path. "I wasn't as patient as I could have been. I...let you have it pretty fast. That wasn't okay, and I should have tried to diffuse the situation."

"How the hell were you supposed to do that? Our first time, *finally,*" he said, drawing that word out in a way that had Grace's pulse hammering, "meeting, and I was hungover and I took it out on you."

"That's besides the point," she said, ignoring the way

Anton's handsome face scrunched up in dismay. She lifted one shoulder. "I owed it to Lou to make sure our first run-in went off without a hitch. No matter your behavior. You've been practically bankrolling Betsy's fancy new facelift."

He looked at her in confusion. "Betsy?"

"Ah, the telescope. Beta, or whatever Lou calls her, is so boring."

Anton hummed and nodded, eyes moving ahead of them to where the rest of the science crew had disappeared. "So I have been. And you think me bringing that ramshackle—"

Grace made a face. "She has character."

"Derelict," he corrected.

"Excuse me, it's called built to last."

Anton snorted. "Practically nonexistent technology specifications."

"I believe that could be termed as old-world charm," Grace said.

Anton took a drink from the bottle. "Only if you use the phrase loosely and liberally."

They turned and began walking down the path once more. Grace opened her mouth, fully intending to wax poetic about Betsy's stalwart virtues, but Anton beat her to the punch.

"You have nothing to apologize for, Grace. I deserved everything you threw my way."

A beat of silence passed before she cleared her throat. "Very true. You did."

Anton sighed with a little grin. "A truthful queen. How refreshing."

"Is it?" Grace sipped her drink, eyes on the man next to her, the man who seemed light years away from the brat she had encountered less than a day before. What would she do now that he was here with her like she'd wanted for months?

"You have no idea. I quite like it."

"That's…" Grace bit her lip, trying to pick her next words with care. "Well, good."

"I'm glad you think that, because I do, too."

"I'm sorry about RED," she said suddenly.

At the mention of the stolen equipment Anton's expression darkened, the happy smile on his face slipping away, and Grace almost swore. What had she been thinking, bringing up RED out of nowhere? She'd meant to show that she remembered, not wipe the smile off his face.

"I just—I'm sorry, I didn't mean to upset you," she said, but Anton waved her off.

"It's alright. No harm, no foul. I mean, you didn't steal it. Shit happens. Just have to move on and learn from it," he said, with a smile that didn't quite meet his eyes, and when he took a long drink from the bottle Grace nearly winced. "I'll take what I learned..apply it somewhere else...like Betsy's jaunt into this century."

Her lips turned up in a half-smile. "I'm still sorry. I didn't mean to bring the energy down. It's just that Lou told me what happened and we hadn't…" Her voice trailed off and she looked away from him, cheeks burning hot at what she hadn't said.

"And I hadn't called to tell you yet," he said, filling in the words she'd stopped herself from saying. He smiled at her when she looked at him in surprise. They stepped out from the trail and into the bustling clearing that served as their party site. "Don't fret. You'll just have to make it up to me."

"Excuse me?" Her mouth went dry at the words, but Anton had already turned toward the party that seemed to be in full swing. The bonfire burned away while their teams worked to assemble s'mores and pass out libations.

Anton shot her a wink and raised his bottle to her glass in a toast. "My queen."

And then the man was gone, slipping away into the crowd that parted like the Red Sea for him, leaving a confused but intrigued Grace in his wake.

CHAPTER FIVE

"The meeting of two personalities is like the contact of two chemical substances: If there is any reaction, both are transformed."

—Carl Jung

"Why do you look like you just saw a gamma ray burst?"

"Huh?" Grace looked to the side to see Lou giving her a considering look. "What are you talking about?"

Lou clasped her hands in front of her and straightened her back like she was giving a book report. "Gamma ray bursts are explosions that are the most energetic—"

"I know what a gamma ray burst is, woman. I'm science-y, okay?" Grace scowled at her friend.

"Sorry, I wasn't sure how much was going on upstairs with that dumb look on your face."

"I do not have a dumb look."

"Do too."

"Well, if I do, it sure as hell isn't my fault," Grace

hissed. "There isn't a woman alive who wouldn't have a dumb look on her face after my little run-in."

Since her encounter with Anton she had set up camp by the fire, making s'mores. The spot by the fire had been perfect for a little brooding over her feelings for Anton, which had her twisted up five ways from Sunday ever since he'd opened his mouth to bark a coffee order at her.

She'd thought she hated him...but now? His apology put her off-kilter. She didn't know how she felt—or what she wanted from him now. The way he looked at her, the effortless way conversation had flowed, the way she'd felt like a live wire beside him.

It had made her want. Want *him*. But that wasn't right...it couldn't be right, could it?

Her eyes darted from the bonfire and landed on Anton. He held court amid the people who surrounded him, the bottle of Moët still dangling from his hand as he laughed with the group.

She swallowed when he raised the bottle to his lips. Her thoughts had just begun to veer south of acceptable when he raised his free hand and wiggled his fingers in a wave. It took a full second of staring for Grace to realize he waved at *her*.

"Fuck," she groaned, giving him a jerky wave. Executing an about-face that her middle school marching band teacher could set a watch to, Grace ran headlong into a smirking Lou.

"Does this little run-in have something to do with a certain visiting astrophysicist you were just daydreaming about?"

"I wasn't daydreaming. I was just lost in my thoughts."

Grace reached over to the table beside her and grabbed a graham cracker. She took a bite and gave Lou a nonchalant shrug. "No idea what you're going on about. How much have you had to drink, boss lady?"

"Not enough to miss your lecherous staring."

Grace rolled her eyes and opened her mouth to retort, but the sound of Anton's voice made her go still as a statue.

"Lecherous staring?" he asked.

Grace shoved the remaining graham cracker in her mouth and sent a silent threat to Lou to speak with care. She glared for all she was worth while she chewed, and grabbed another cracker for effect.

If she was eating, then she couldn't get into too much trouble. It was science.

"Sorry?" Lou stepped toward Anton with a quickness that showed she had, indeed, received her telepathic warning. Grace made a mental note to get the kind of pastries Lou loved for breakfast the next day.

"I heard you say 'lecherous staring'. Who or what are we talking about?"

Lou waved a flippant hand. "This and that," she said, taking a sip of her drink.

"This and that?" Anton raised an eyebrow and looked over Lou's shoulder to Grace, who chewed her graham cracker with the intensity and focus of a chipmunk.

"Hungry?" Anton nodded at the other graham cracker she still clutched in her hand.

"Grace has an insatiable appetite for graham crackers," Lou said, prompting a glare from Grace. "What?" Lou raised a shoulder in mock innocence.

Grace scratched off getting breakfast pastries for Lou from her to-do list.

"Do you know the origin of the graham cracker?" Anton asked in a voice far too sensual to be used in polite conversation. Grace's spidey-sense tingled at the simple question.

This was a trap. She could feel it.

But how?

"No. What is it?" Lou asked, walking straight into the trap Grace hadn't figured out.

"These little culinary experiments were invented by a man who thought it could be used to stop lust."

Grace stopped chewing. She was beginning to understand where Anton was going. By Odin, she was in trouble.

"What? That's crazy." Lou laughed, giving the cracker Anton held in his hand a skeptical look.

"Pseudoscience is crazy." Anton tossed the cracker in his hand and caught it with a grin. "Bland food was supposed to stop sexual desire." His eyes slid from the cracker to Grace's stuffed cheeks, and he tilted his head to the side. "Sex clouds the mind. Makes you do rash things. The original version of the graham cracker was like sawdust, which was the perfect antidote to any lustful actions, or so they thought. What do you think?"

Lou shrugged. "Well—"

"Doctor Wright!" a voice called out, and the trio turned to see Anton's assistant waving a hand at them. "We need you over here on the double!"

"I—what?" Lou spluttered as the woman wrapped an

arm around her and spun her away, toward the group at the far side of the clearing. "What's going on?"

"You'll see. Very important science business. We need your expertise, if you would be so kind."

"Well, all right."

The women walked away, but not before Grace caught sight of Anton's assistant giving him a high-five on her way past.

Grace swallowed her graham cracker and took a hasty sip of her champagne. She was going to need all the liquid courage she could handle if she wanted to make it out of this alive, or with any semblance of professionalism still intact.

Anton Kovalev was up to no good.

"Now, where were we?" Anton asked, stepping close to her.

Grace eyed the man and took a step back. "What was that?"

"What was what?"

"I saw the high five," she said, crossing her arms.

Anton smiled, his eyes on the bonfire in front of them. "Someone had to send mother away."

"What's your game, Kovalev?"

He snorted and gave her a sidelong look. "Kovalev. Never been called that by a woman, let alone a queen. I like it."

"Answer the question, please."

"No game, Grace."

Grace raised the graham cracker in front of her and gave it a shake. "Really? No game? Then what was all that talk about lust and sex?"

"I was merely sharing the interesting and highly unexpected origin story of the graham cracker. An entirely relevant discussion, given our s'mores shindig."

Opting to say nothing, Grace refilled her glass from one of the bottles on the table. She took her time, holding the bottle just so and angling her cup as she poured. All the while she felt Anton's watchful gaze on her. When she finished, he held up his bottle to her in a toast.

"Cheers," he said with a wink.

"Cheers," Grace echoed, tapping her cup to his bottle.

The pair drank, their eyes on each other.

"Where'd you learn that stuff about graham crackers?" Grace asked, breaking the heavy silence.

"I had a very strange and religious uncle I spent summers with when I was younger."

She laughed. "And he taught you the history of graham crackers, why?"

"Well, I was a very curious and energetic teenager, you see."

"Meaning?"

Anton blew out an exasperated sigh. "Meaning that he made me eat the damn things for breakfast, lunch, and dinner, after he caught me kissing the pastor's daughter one Sunday."

Grace's eyes widened. "Was it before or after church?" she whispered.

"Before. Made more sense that way. The repenting and all that, you see, made it a very convenient arrangement for everyone involved."

"You did not!" She choked with laughter. She turned to

see a wistful look in Anton's dark eyes as he stared into the fire.

"Oh, but I did." He shrugged and took another drink from his bottle. "Sally McMathers was her name. And what a summer it was."

"You rake," she accused, but her tone was teasing. It was so easy to imagine Anton as an unruly teenager dining on graham crackers for every meal for a round of heavy petting. She grinned and pointed at the cracker he still held. "I don't expect you'll be making any s'mores tonight, then?"

Anton tossed his graham cracker into the fire. "I can barely look at the things without getting flashbacks of being horny every waking hour of the day."

"Now there's a picture."

"Is it?" he asked, and she almost kicked herself at the interest she heard. He wanted to know exactly what she thought about him being horny.

She took another hasty sip of her drink and cleared her throat.

"I, ah, well," she stammered, cheeks flushing under his attention. Damn the man, he knew very well what he was doing. There was no way this wasn't a trap, and she had practically somersaulted into it. This was what she got for having champagne with only s'mores in her stomach. Clearing her throat, she did her best to recover from her misstep. "I mean, if you're into that sort of thing."

"Which is what?"

"You," she said with a roll of her eyes.

Anton chuckled and raised his bottle to his lips. "Which you are."

She blanched and whirled around to face him. “Excuse me?”

He said nothing at her outburst, but gave a little tut and shook his head.

“What?” She crossed her arms and stared him down.

“I see the way you look at me,” he said matter-of-factly. “The way you sound on the phone with me.” It was the tone of a man used to being looked at. Used to getting attention from women.

She bristled at it. He wasn’t the only one who could use shock tactics and get away with it.

“Yeah, well, you look at me too,” she shot back.

“I do.”

“And you wanna talk about the phone? You’re all super breathy on the phone. Like a phone se—” She froze, the words drying up on her tongue. “What do you mean, you do.”

“I mean, you’re right. I do look at you. You’re beautiful.”

Her eyes widened and she gulped. “Oh.”

Anton rocked back on his heels. “Oh,” he parroted back with a cheeky grin.

“Is that why you’re being nice to me?” she asked, narrowing her eyes.

“What?” He gave her a sharp look. “What do you mean?”

“Well, I mean, your apology…I just thought...” She waved a hand, her voice trailing off at the look of disbelief on his face telling her that she’d erred in her assumption.

“I apologized to you because you deserved it. It was

only right, as I was in the wrong. I'm not—Grace, I'm not being nice to you because I'm attracted to you."

"That's good," she said, looking down at her feet. It was too hard to meet his eyes.

"Quite," Anton murmured, and raised the bottle of champagne to his lips. He tipped it back, draining the last of it in a long gulp. He set the bottle on the table and then nodded to the outskirts of the clearing.

"That doesn't mean I'm not attracted to you. Care to walk with me?"

"Love to."

The response escaped her before she even had time to process, and she swallowed hard, choosing to blame the champagne and s'mores she'd inhaled for dinner.

When she fell into step beside Anton and their fingers brushed, she knew it wouldn't have mattered if she ate an entire box of graham crackers, because not even their supposed medicinal origins could have dampened what she felt.

She chanced a look at him and jumped when she found him look at her with an intensity she couldn't quite place, for the sole reason that a look like this had never been directed at her. Grace was the best friend, the one baking a cake and offering a warm plate of lasagna when a friend had a bad day; never had she been the focus of a look like that.

They walked in silence and Grace had only begun to wonder where they headed when Anton steered them toward the brightly lit path leading back to the tram cars. At least she wouldn't have to add worrying about keeping her footing in the near darkness.

“So…” Anton tucked his hands into his pocket. The sounds of laughter and talking faded behind them.

“So,” Grace echoed.

“Now you know I’m attracted to you.”

She nodded. “And you know I’m attracted to you.”

“How very liberating. Don’t you think?”

The gravel crushed underfoot, and for a moment Grace said nothing, savoring the quiet of the night. A gentle breeze blew her hair around her shoulders, and she relaxed in the stillness of the forest, all her cares on hold for the time being.

“I suppose that’s one way to look at it,” she agreed, “but now what?”

He came to a stop. They had made their way back to the tram cars and stood at the base of the trail, the twinkling path at their backs. “Funny you should ask.”

“And why is that?”

“Because, I, my lovely queen, have a proposition for you to consider.”

She tilted her head to the side. “And what might that be?”

“That we have a fling,” he said.

She should have expected nothing less from a well-known playboy. It didn’t matter that she’d thought she knew him. What did you really learn from someone from months of emails and a precious handful of phone calls, anyhow?

She should have known what a man like him might want, asking her to walk alone on a fairy light path. Should have known that it wouldn’t mean to him what it did to her.

She swallowed and met Anton's gaze with an unwavering stare. The forest sighed and breathed around them, making her forget that they were only feet away from a roaring bonfire party.

In this moment there was only them. Nothing else mattered. Nothing but Anton's question was important.

"A fling or an affair?" she asked after a moment.

He gave her a half-smile. "Perhaps a mix of both? A tryst?"

She turned away from him and looked out into the dark. "And why would I agree to do that?" she asked, her heart squeezing so tight she was surprised she hadn't hit the forest floor.

Why did she always fall for this type of man? Anton had been wrapped in prettier packaging than the rest, but here it was, all the same.

A man who wanted her, but only for a moment.

"I'm a lot of fun," he said.

"So I've heard," Grace quipped, earning her a sigh.

"It's all lies, you know," he told her, his voice a touch too earnest for her liking. It had no place in a conversation like this, asking her to be a fling.

"I find that hard to believe when you're proposing we have a—what did you call it?" She snapped her fingers in recollection and looked back at him over her shoulder. "Ah, yes, an affair."

Anton wagged a finger. "Ah, ah, ah, that was not my word choice. I said a tryst, which is known the world over to be a far classier engagement. We could even term it a rendezvous, if it suited your mood. Keep it interesting."

"Still doesn't make me believe the rumors about you aren't true," she pointed out.

"I can see how that might paint me in a certain light, but what I'm proposing between the two of us would be civil, consensual, and respectful."

"For how long?"

He raised an eyebrow. "How long what?"

She crossed her arms. "How long would this civil, consensual, and respectful rendezvous go on for?"

"The duration of my stay in Geneva," he answered, and then said, "or it could be even shorter, if you wanted."

She didn't want to hear the answer, but she asked her question anyhow. "And then what?"

"Then we go on our separate ways an—"

"And just pretend it never happened?" she interrupted him, barely able to conceal her irritation. Why she was mad she didn't know. She stepped back from him and he moved quickly, trying to close the distance he could see her putting between them.

"Well, yes, that is generally how these things go," he explained gently.

"That's crazy," she said with a snort, emboldened by the champagne.

"How so?"

"You don't just...sleep with someone and then pretend it never happened."

"You...don't?"

Grace shook her head and took another step away from him with a glare. "Of course not. Who does that? This is real life, not some romcom movie. People don't have relationships with determined dates of completion.

How can you go from sleeping with someone on a Friday to cutting them out on a Monday? That would be actual torture."

Anton looked puzzled. "It would?"

She threw her arms out at her sides and spun around to face him. "Yes. If you like someone—if there's—we have chemistry, okay? From day one, there was something there. I nearly died the first time you called me."

A smile lit up his face. "Really?"

"Yes. Really," she gritted out, and then sucked in a deep breath, plowing on ahead before she lost her nerve. "We've got chemistry by the bucketful. And if there's chemistry and you like them and sleep with them, then feelings happen. Feelings make things complicated, and you don't just walk away easy-peasy from that, okay?"

"You..." He rubbed a hand against the back of his neck. "I mean, you have feelings for me?"

"Well, *yeah*."

"Oh." Anton blinked and shook his head like he had just been hit with a blunt object—and maybe he had. It wasn't like sort-of-declarations of feelings were an everyday occurrence. "Oh, wow. Just...I...wow."

From another man that stuttering, stumbling string of words might have done her in and made her turn tail and run back to the bonfire, or maybe even push her to take the tram back down the mountain in horror...but now, with him, it was different. His voice was filled with a sort of awe that made her go still.

The look in his eyes was reverent.

They stared at each other for a long beat while Grace tried to make sense of Anton's reaction.

"I see." He rubbed a hand over his jaw. "Then tell me, what do people do?" He took a step toward her, and then another, and this time Grace didn't backpedal, didn't look for an escape or a way to put space between them. This time she waited for him, leaned into him almost, as he came closer.

"They get in relationships and see what happens."

"And then?" He took another step toward her until they stood only inches apart. She could feel the heat of his body on hers, and she blushed.

"Well, I don't...I don't know, all right? No one knows when they start a relationship. Sometimes it works out and sometimes it doesn't, but that's the risk. You don't get to wrap things up in a nice little bow on some arbitrary date and move on like nothing happened. You let your walls down and pray to Odin they don't hurt you because it's worth it."

He took a deep breath. "So what does that mean in relation to my proposal exactly?"

"It means that I have a counteroffer," Grace said.

"I'm listening."

"Well, we already know that I...that I like you, so you know what? I propose a relationship," she blurted out.

"A what?!"

"A relationship. *A real one.* None of this funny half-assed stuff, none of that millennial 'we're just talking' bull. A real bona fide relationship." She pinned him with a look and tossed her pink hair over her shoulder.

"I've never really been good at that," he said, voice quiet.

She shot him a smoking pair of finger guns. "No time like the present, as they say."

Anton gave her a half-smile. "They do say that, don't they?"

"Verily." She worried her bottom lip as she watched him consider her words. He was silent for another beat before he nodded to himself.

"Right, then," he said, turning to her. His dark eyes slid up her body with a deliberate slowness that made her breath catch.

Holy hell.

He was actually going to do it, wasn't he?

"I accept," he declared.

"Really?" Grace squeaked as he began to reach for her. Her breath stilled in her chest when his hands settled on her hips, warm fingers rubbing against her sides.

"Truly," he said, drawing her close to him with a gentle tug on her jeans, "but for it to be official, we have one more thing to do."

"What's that?" Grace turned her face up to look at him he closed the space between them. She was pressed up against him, chest-to-chest and toe-to-toe, as she waited for him to speak.

Anton reached out a finger and tipped her chin up. "Seal it with a kiss. Only way to be on the up-and-up. I'm not going into this with you taking advantage of me by not signing off on the deal."

"Yes, let's notarize this agreement." Her eyes had already fluttered closed in anticipation of the kiss.

He chuckled. "A deal's a deal. We are in a bona fide relationship."

Grace bobbed her head, eyes still closed. "Now make it real official-like and kiss me, sailor. I've been waiting for this moment for months. Lay it on me."

"However long you waited for this," he whispered, his lips brushing against hers in the barest caress, "I have waited for far longer."

And he kissed her again, this time in earnest. His hands were warm and strong on her sides as he deepened the kiss, his tongue and lips far gentler than Grace would have expected, but she found she liked the delicacy in his touch.

Odin, it had been too long since someone had handled her with such care. She was so lost in the way he touched her that she didn't process his words immediately...and then she did.

I have waited for far longer.

How long had he wanted to do this?

A moan caught in her throat at the thought of it. How could this man keep changing how she viewed him? It was almost as dizzying as the way he caressed her, fingers just ghosting over her skin, tracing her while he devoured her mouth.

Tilting her head further back to give him better access to her mouth, she reached up and finally did what she had been longing to do since that first phone call had set her heart racing. She ran her fingers through his tresses and swooned at how silky-soft his hair felt between her fingers.

Anton groaned at the scrape of her nails against his scalp, and suddenly the kiss turned into something different. The energy changed from sweet to steamy in the span of a heartbeat.

It wasn't a tentative first kiss any longer.

It felt so good to be wanted.

She nipped his bottom lip, a nanosecond away from climbing him like a tree, when an explosion boomed through the trees, causing them both to freeze.

"Gracie?!" Lou's voice rang through the night, causing Grace to groan and close her eyes with a wince. "Where are you?! I've lost control of them!"

"Mom's calling," Anton teased, leaning close to her. He had a smile on his face that warmed her like sunshine, and Grace bit her lip at the feel of his warm hands on her body. All she wanted was to stay exactly where she was and repeat their kiss about one or 2.5 million more times.

Alas, she had a science hoard to wrangle, and apparently there were explosions?

Not that she was surprised.

Heaven help them when she figured out what was going on. She'd known it was a risk to have open flames and alcohol near so many little science-makers.

"We should go back..." Grace sighed when she heard Lou shout her name again, this time closer to their hiding spot. She slipped out of Anton's arms and moved to head back to the bonfire. She felt the world spinning around her from the kiss Anton had just laid on her, but at least the explozapalooza gave her something to ground herself with.

What did it mean when explosions at bonfires had a calming effect on her? Grace shook her head. Nevermind —she didn't want to know.

Anton slipped his hand into hers and tugged her back to him and all her thoughts came to a screeching halt. She looked down at their entwined fingers and swallowed hard. She'd been right—he had sensational hands.

"I don't know a lot about stable romantic relationships, but I do know hand-holding is customary when returning from a romp," he said, holding up their linked fingers.

"That wasn't a romp." She rolled her eyes, grinning despite herself.

"Let me call it a romp. I need some semblance of order," he said with a pinched look on his face, but the expression vanished when she pressed a quick kiss to his cheek.

"Okay, it was a romp," she whispered, lips against his cheek.

"Thank you," he said, running his free hand through his hair and giving it a vigorous tousle so it looked well and properly ruined. "Now then, if anyone asks, you were thoroughly debauched, understand?"

"Deal. By all accounts, I'm practically a fallen woman. Someone get me to a nunnery. Should I mess up my hair, too?"

"No, of course not. I am a gentle lover. Everyone knows this. I'd never mess my date's hair up in public."

"Gee thanks, Kovalev."

CHAPTER SIX

*"*LIFE NEED NOT BE EASY, *provided only that it is not empty."*
—Lise Meitner

ANTON BLINKED in surprise at the scene of utter chaos greeting his and Grace's return to the party.

The energy was off, tense now instead of merry. This was definitely *not* a party anymore. When he'd asked Grace for a walk, he hadn't anticipated this kind of carnage. They'd been gone for all of twenty minutes, for Pete's sake. He cautioned a look at Grace.

"What do you think happened?" he asked her.

She tucked a pink lock of hair behind an ear and shook her head. "I don't know, but I don't like this. I think I just heard an intern say their eyebrows are gone. When I said mayhem, I didn't mean literally. Come on, I need to find Lou and sort this out."

Finding Lou wasn't a problem. Not when the tiny

woman came barreling out of the crowd and straight toward them.

Lou threw herself into Grace's arms. "Thank god you're here! They've lost their minds. I blame the altitude."

"Whoa, slow down." Grace pulled back to look at her friend. "We heard an explosion. Please tell me it was not us."

"It was so us." Lou shook her head. "Or, I mean, them. It was them." She gestured at the chaos around her. "I'm innocent, I tell you. My only crime is thinking this horde could be civil."

"What exactly happened?" Anton ventured, looking around and seeing that his own science team was noticeably excited. He frowned when he saw Mindy grab a scientist by the collar and shake a clipboard at him.

Things were bad if the clipboard was out.

Lou flung her arms wide. "They blew up the bonfire."

"Come again?" Grace stepped forward and held a hand up. "I don't think I quite understood what you just said."

"I don't know what's so hard to understand. They blew the bonfire up."

Grace whirled on the milling scientists with a downright murderous look in her eyes.

"What the hell?" she roared.

Anton was honestly impressed that she had such an ungodly sound in her. A silence descended on the clearing with all the gravitas of Thor's hammer, and no one dared speak a word as Grace sucked in a deep breath.

"I did this out of the goodness of my heart, and do you know why?" she asked them, her voice quiet now. When no one answered, she continued on with a sweeping glare, hands on her hips.

"I did it because I love you all. Even you, New York team. I mean, I don't know you, but you're my people, and do you know why?"

At this, a scientist made of far sterner stuff than Anton had assumed stepped forward. "Because you're, ah, the lab queen?" they supplied with a smile Anton assumed was meant to be placating.

"You're damn right," she yelled, pointing a finger at the scientist and marching forward. "But if you think for one second I'm going to tolerate a lab war resembling the previous one circa *last year,* then you've got another thing coming. Do you get me? I've stared into the depths of space with naught but a hot pocket and my love for this woman to keep my wits about me and my sanity intact." She nodded at Lou, who sipped her beer with a bland expression on her face; this was, Anton supposed, old hat to Lou, after all.

"If you think you're going to do what I know you're plotting then brace yourself, because I've got a budget five times yours and no social hang-ups holding me back when it comes to keeping peace and order in my labs."

"Holy shit," Mindy breathed, her eyes wide as she watched Grace launch into another tirade that would make Napoleon proud, "she's terrifying."

Anton nodded, his eyes following Grace as she marched around the clearing with all the pomp of a queen. He'd gotten off with a slap on the wrist for the way he'd behaved on their first meeting.

"I know."

"It's magnificent. I approve of you dating her."

Anton balked, eyes snapping to Mindy. "Wait, what? How do you know that already?"

Mindy shrugged. "It's my job to know what you're getting yourself into, and I approve. Besides, you've been mooning over her for months. It's time you did the deed and got some of that energy out. It's not healthy, with the hours you've been keeping."

"Mindy…" Anton groaned, covering his face with a hand. "This is like getting the birds and the bees talk from my mom."

She scowled. "I am not your mom."

"Also, let me remind you all! What's the first rule of Lab Wars?!" Grace demanded from the group with a raised eyebrow.

"Don't get caught," someone yelled.

"Wrong," she yelled, "it's don't talk about Lab Wars, and you know why? It doesn't exist. Don't even think about it! Don't breathe in its general direction, and don't fantasize about it, and don't write about it on your damn science blogs. I swear to god, if you ruin another family outing I will turn this campfire right around and take us all home."

Lou barked out a laugh, which only served to add to Grace's consternation. "What? I can laugh. We're blood-sisters. You have to love me." Grace glared at her, prompting a half-hearted mutter of "I'm in charge around here, you know."

"Thin ice, boss lady. Thin freaking ice," Grace muttered, pinching her fingers together.

Lou's lips turned down in a pout, but the scientist said nothing as Grace continued to eyeball the line of assembled scientists.

"Consider this your first and final warning about Lab Wars. I will not be having a repeat of it from last year. Not on my watch, and not against the visiting team. I'll take you all on and you'll lose. Don't make me cut off your coffee."

A gasp went up from the group of party-goers, but Grace continued speaking.

"I'll do it. I'll drown you in so much decaf you won't be able to go on your little science benders, capisce?" Grace punctuated the end of her sentence with a snap of her fingers. Anton had never seen a group of people scramble to agree faster than this stammering and all-but-bowing group of scientists.

Geniuses that they were, they knew when they'd been beaten.

Anton shoved his hands in his pocket and ambled up to Grace as she held court, receiving heartfelt apologies and promises of better behavior in exchange for caffeine.

"And don't think I don't know that you masterminded this, Elisha." Grace jabbed a finger at a willowy scientist with a pile of box braids. The woman fiddled with one braid and gave Grace a little shrug.

"I have no idea what you're referring to, Gracie," she demurred, one corner of her lips turning up into a smile. "This wasn't me."

"Your lips say no, but your hips say yes," Grace muttered, arms crossed as Elisha skirted past, but not before pressing a kiss to Grace's cheek. "Play nice with the

New York team," Grace sighed when Elisha drew away with a wink.

"Please caffeinate me," Elisha called over her shoulder.

"Half-caff! Nothing more," Grace barked out, but there was a smile on her face, especially when Elisha's disgruntled moan hit her ears.

"Kids these days," Anton said, coming to stand beside Grace.

"They grow up so fast, you know?" Grace sighed.

"I SWEAR BY ODIN, these antics are going to drive me to an early grave." Grace stared out at the lab from where she sat beside Lou.

The pair drank their morning coffee while the labs came to life around them, the scientists nursing the coffees Grace had distributed in relative silence—mostly because she was certain they were trying to decipher if they were one of the unlucky ones who had been served decaf.

"There's no rhyme or reason to it. Half are leaded and the other half unleaded. Enjoy," Grace had announced that morning when she deposited the three stacks of coffee onto the table at the center of the room. Normally, she made sure to get a cup into each and every science minion's hot little hand, but today?

No. Not after their stunt to bring Lab Wars back.

It was self-serve, and with the added threat of decaf.

"You're cruel," Elisha sighed, walking by with a cup in

her hand. She sipped with a grimace. "Don't think I don't know that you just gave us all decaf."

"Did I?" Grace tapped her chin before she drank from her own cup. "I mean, it tastes normal to me. What do you think, Lou?"

"Completely normal," Lou chimed in, raising her cup in solidarity.

Elisha rolled her eyes. "That's just because she's the boss and you would never under-caffeinate her."

"I have to," Grace replied, already paging through a stack of paperwork that needed her attention. "She fakes her naps, and you know how she gets when she hasn't slept. It's either coffee or we all die."

Elisha pouted but said nothing more and turned on her heel, stalking back to her workstation where several other scientists sat and stared at their coffees with frowns.

Lou chuckled and leaned back in her chair. "Be careful or the natives might revolt."

"I'd like to see them try," Grace murmured, her pen moving over the forms.

"How did things go with you and Anton?"

Grace's hand froze. "What do you mean?"

"You two disappeared together."

"Did we?" Grace resumed signing the papers and took her time arranging the stack on her desk. When Lou didn't respond she sighed and looked up at her friend to see the smaller woman wiggling her eyebrows at her.

Eyebrow wiggling was Lou's go-to response when anything remotely sexual occured. Grace was certain she'd been doing it nonstop while she waited for Grace to look at her.

“That a new face workout regimen to stay limber?”

Lou gasped but kept wiggling her eyebrows. “You know what this is. This is my ‘you’re being racy and semi-indecent with Anton’ face.”

“Am not,” Grace argued, though she wasn’t sure why she denied it. She had proposed for him to date her, after all—a bona fide relationship with all the trimmings—so it was a little too late to deny it.

“Are too.” Lou increased her eyebrow wiggling to maximum capacity.

“Your face is going to get stuck like that,” Grace pointed out.

“Good. Then you’ll always know what I think of you,” Lou shot back, but she stopped wiggling her eyebrows. She raised a hand to her forehead and massaged it. “Ow. That is an actual workout.”

Grace shook her head with a laugh. “Look, I don’t know what you—”

“Don’t play coy with me. Mindy already told me the two of you are dating. I can’t believe you didn’t tell me first. I knew there was something going on with all those emails—”

“Keep your tiny voice down.” Grace’s hand shot out, grabbing Lou by the shoulder and jerking her close, so close that Lou slid partway across the table.

“Holy shit. I didn’t know you were this strong.” Lou blinked and looked over the table as her feet dangled off the floor. “I also didn’t know I liked being manhandled. That’s new.”

Grace let go of her shoulder. “Stop that. I’m being serious.”

"So am I," Lou pointed out, pushing herself up.

"That's it. Decaf tomorrow."

"What? No! You're the one kink-shaming me. Why am I being punished?"

Grace jabbed a finger at her, voice indignant. "You brought it on yourself."

"Pfft. So this is how you get when you have a boyfriend. I see how it is."

Grace groaned, a blush spreading over her cheeks. "Zip it, you. What the hell did Mindy tell you? I haven't even gotten things situated with Anton."

"What do you mean?" Lou slid into the seat next to Grace with a frown. "Mindy said it was a legitimate relationship. What's to sort out? You guys even kissed on it, from what I heard."

"Well, I mean, yeah, I guess we did seal the deal…"

"But what?"

"We got interrupted by the science pyros over there." Grace jerked her chin at Elisha's table. "She thinks I'm not onto her but joke's on her. I overcaffeinated her coffee."

"You what?" Lou laughed, nearly choking on the sip she had just taken.

"She's drinking coffee concentrate. That's why it tastes awful, not because it's decaf. If I know Elisha, she's plotting, but at the rate she's drinking down the coffee she'll crash by lunchtime, and then I can have peace and quiet."

"Is that ethical?" Lou asked.

"I don't care what the ethics are. I need order to work, and let it be a lesson to them about Lab Wars. I'm not doing that again."

"That was a very trying and dark time for the labs,"

Lou agreed with a sigh, but then she sat up with a jerk. "Hey. Don't change the subject here. I'm focused on what happened between you and Anton. Why is it that you're not sure you're dating when even his own assistant is ready to monogram your initials together on an agenda cover?"

"She is not," Grace gasped.

Lou wiggled her eyebrows. "Isn't she?"

"I hate you."

Lou tapped the desk. "Whatever. Spill."

"Fine." Grace hunched over her coffee cup and blew out a sigh. "I may or may not have dared Anton to date me."

"What do you mean dare?"

"Okay, that's not the right word. It just felt like a dare because he propositioned me with a tryst—"

"He what? I specifically told him no sex romps." Lou slammed her hand on the desk with enough force to shake it.

"Again, keep it down. Elisha hasn't passed out yet, and the last thing I need is her leading a revolt while you're talking about forbidden sex romps."

"Fine, fine, I'll shut up. Continue."

"Thank you." Grace settled back in her chair and cleared her throat. "Anton was being his usual playboy rake self, but I went into the woods with him because, yes, he's attractive as hell and, yes, I've had a crush on him for months." She paused, rolling her eyes at Lou, who mouthed *I knew it* at her, and continued on. "That's when he ambushed me with the tryst proposal and I—well, I counter-offered."

"Counter-offered how?" Lou asked when Grace didn't continue.

"I told him I wasn't going to do a rendezvous with a time limit and that, well, if he wanted to get in my pants then he was going to have to date me. Like for real."

Lou's eyes widened. "And he agreed? Just like that?"

"Yes, just like that, but then Firestarter over there blew up the bonfire and we got interrupted, which is why I'm saying I don't exactly know how much I'm dating him. For all I know we are *tinily* dating."

"What does that even mean?"

"Bigly is like a lot. The whole thing. Tinily is maybe we text or get pizza when we're drunk. Fool around or something."

Lou gaped but said nothing.

"What?"

Lou snapped her mouth shut with an audible click. "Look, it's very bigly, or whatever. There's no tinily. If he told Mindy, then I'm saying *very* bigly is a good guess."

"I guess so," Grace muttered, resting her chin in her palm. How they'd gone from friends to not and then straight past friends to something more in the span of a week had her head spinning. It was thrilling to think of the possibilities, but how was it true when she still couldn't believe she'd been so daring as to ask for it?

Her eyes jerked up to Lou's face when her friend made a sound somewhere between choking and grunting.

"What is it?" Grace asked, already leaning toward Lou to slap her back in case of a freak choking accident. It wouldn't do to have her big-brained friend keel over from choking on her own spit.

Lou inclined her head behind Grace with a laugh. "The fact that he's coming over here with flowers seems like another good indicator that you're 100% dating Anton. Bigly dating."

Grace's eyes widened. "What?" she squeaked. "Flowers?"

"Lots of them. Expensive ones too," Lou replied, sliding away from her friend with a wink. "I'll just leave you alone for some privacy, so you two can do datey things."

"Wait!" Grace tried to make a swipe for Lou's arm but the woman danced away, coffee in hand, and didn't so much as spare her best friend a look as she practically skipped past Anton with a knowing look on her face.

Grace made to bolt after her, but froze when she caught sight of the bouquet making its way through the lab towards her. It was practically a bouquet with legs, as it dwarfed Anton's frame so that only his legs and feet were visible.

"Holy shit," she breathed, eyes widening when she realized that Lou had been right. When a man brought you a bouquet half his size, then you were dating.

That had to be written down somewhere in the *How To Boyfriend Properly* instruction manual. Was there a manual? If there was, then she should really look into procuring her own copy. It figured Anton would have already memorized the manual and left her scrambling to catch up.

When the bouquet with legs came to a stop in front of Grace, she set her pen down and craned her neck, trying to get a look at Anton's face, but everywhere she looked there was just another exotic flower.

"Hello?" she said.

"I got you these," came the muffled reply before Anton shifted the bouquet to the side and popped his head out.

"They're… I just—they're very big," Grace said with wide eyes.

Anton sighed. "They're too big, aren't they?"

"No, no! I love them. Thank you so much. No one's ever gotten me flowers before."

"What?" He pursed his lips and maneuvered the flowers onto the desk in front of her. "What do you mean?"

She ducked her head, one finger going out to toy with a lily petal. "I've never been given flowers before."

His hands went to his hips. "I absolutely should have gotten you the bigger one."

"There was a bigger one?"

"Of course there was, but I think it was reserved for the likes of partners who forget their anniversaries, buy one-ply toilet paper, make the family give up carbs, and so on," he told her with a shrug.

Grace pulled a face. "I don't think there are enough flowers in the city to make up for no carbs or one-ply."

"Agreed. I hope I never do any of those things."

She grinned at the solemn tone in his voice. "Thank you for the flowers."

Anton smiled and hitched a hip against the lab table. "You're very welcome. It seemed the right way to begin day one of, well, this..." His voice trailed off and he furrowed his brow as he searched for the right word.

"Us," Grace supplied.

"Us," Anton agreed, and then gestured toward the bouquet with a sweep of his arms. "Is this a good start? I mean, there isn't a manual to consult, which let me tell you, as a man who lives and dies by research, is a highly uncomfortable situation to be put in."

Grace bit back a laugh and relaxed against her seat. It was nice to know that even a renowned playboy was at a loss when it came to functioning in an actual relationship.

"I'd say you're off to a more than adequate start." She tucked a lock of pink hair behind her ear and cautioned a look around the lab. She bit back a grin when she saw every woman in the lab staring at Anton with heart eyes. Elisha pumped her fist at Grace while she mouthed *you go, girl* to her.

"In fact, I'd say that the entire lady population in this lab agrees with me on how above and beyond your efforts are in the boyfriend game."

He shot her a wink. "I'll have you know that I've always been an overachiever."

"Is that so?"

"Top of my class." He waved a hand. "Dean's list, the whole shebang. You're very lucky, you know. I've got it all in writing."

"I'll make sure to have your credentials apostilled by the end of day, Mr. Kovalev."

"That could take some time, so why don't I just show you?"

"Show me?"

He nodded, hands going to his pockets. "Mm, the flowers were just the first stop on the boyfriend train."

"What's the final destination of the locomotive, then?"

"Brunch. That's a thing couples do. I know this for a fact, manual or not, from copious amounts of movie-watching and the sort."

Grace nodded and bounced out of her seat. "Farmer's markets are next up on the couple to-do list, aren't they?"

Anton laughed and offered his arm to her. "Did you look ahead on the itinerary or something? Because that is not playing fair."

She hooked her arm through his and followed him toward the lab doors. "I thought we both agreed that there's no manual, which means that I can kinda do whatever I want." She paused and bit her lip, glancing around the lab as they reached the front door. There was still so much to be done for Lou's research, and there was an entire data set she hadn't even touched. Grace tugged on his arm to pull Anton short of the door.

"Wait. I don't think I can go."

Anton raised an eyebrow. "Why not?"

"There's just so much to do here." She jerked a thumb over her shoulder and stepped closer to him. "I gave them all decaf," she whispered. "This place is a ticking time bomb and I can't leave Lou to deal with it on her own. She hasn't even been taking her scheduled naps, you know?"

"What does that mean?"

"It means that we are one tiny science bender away from her deciding that she needs equipment capable of projecting her consciousness on an intergalactic level. Do you know how close that woman is to becoming an actual supervillain?"

Anton huffed out a laugh. "You know what? After she roughed me up, I can see it."

"I did not rough you up." Lou came to stand beside them with her arms crossed. "I put the fear of truth and justice into you." She cut her eyes to Grace. "Which basically makes me Wonder Woman, the exact opposite of a supervillain."

Grace held up her hands. "Whatever you say, boss lady."

"Get out of here, okay? I can handle the science horde for a few hours."

"And what do you promise me if I go?" Grace asked, crossing her arms to match her friend's stance.

Lou rolled her eyes and blew out an exasperated sigh before she held up a hand. "I swear not to build technology that I intend to use for selfish gain," she said. "I won't even go near Beta while you're out."

"Betsy," Grace corrected, and then she nodded at her friend. "Keep going. What else are you not going to do?"

"Fiiiine," Lou said, the sound making Grace laugh and Anton take a step back. "I promise not to break rules three through seven of our science no-go list."

"See what I mean about her? We are about this close," Grace said, pinching her fingers together, "from her trying to take over the world."

"I'd be a fair ruler."

"You once threatened to build a shrink ray," Grace reminded her.

"That was one time!"

"Uh-huh." Grace put her hands on her hips and looked

back at Anton. She wanted to go to brunch, but if she did she ran the risk of coming back to mayhem and a destroyed lab… But then again, she'd left Lou alone before and things had been fine.

But that also hadn't been on the brink of a Lab War.

"I want you to go have fun. We can even put Elisha in charge, if you want."

Grace balked. "How does that make things any better for my peace of mind? She's even worse than you."

"I have a solution," Anton piped up, cell phone in his hand. "I know a fearsome warrior up to the task of ensuring law and order in these labs."

"Oh?" Grace said.

"I get no respect around here," Lou muttered. "You threaten to build one tiny little shrink ray and you never live it down."

"Get your person here and fast," Grace said to Anton.

"She's already here." Anton nodded at his assistant, who breezed into the lab with an almost bored look on her face.

"Are these the science people I'm watching?" Mindy asked.

"Yes, and the tiny one is the worst."

"Excuse me? Technically, the science people are them, not me," Lou told her.

Grace crossed her arms and gave Mindy a look. "She's lying. Watch her at all costs. She has plans to be a supervillain."

"Got it." Mindy nodded and made a note on her tablet. "Lou is evil and requires supervision."

"Precisely," Grace said.

"That's a gross exaggeration. Evil?" Lou threw up her hands. "I'm mischievous at best. Evil? No way. Mindy, you know me. You know I'm telling the truth."

"Shrink ray, Lou." Grace wagged a finger at her.

"That was one time!"

CHAPTER SEVEN

"I NEED *physics more than I need friends."*
—J. Robert Oppenheimer

"DO you think they'll be okay?" Grace twisted her fingers and turned her head, looking behind her in the direction of the labs.

Anton had whisked her off in a waiting car and driven with the speed only someone familiar with Geneva could manage.

It had been nice to get out of the labs.

From the moment their plane had touched down all those months ago, Grace was sad to say that much of her daylight waking hours had been spent sequestered away in the labs, with only occasional evening jaunts to the bars with Lou.

This was nice in the sort of way that filled her stomach with butterflies and made her pulse speed up when Anton took her hand and led her up the sidewalk to a trendy but cozy eatery.

"They're fine. Stop worrying. Mindy is the best in the business," he said, holding the door open for her.

"And what business is that?"

"That whole keeping-depraved-and-destructive-scientists-semi-functional business. She works with me, and let me tell you, I practically have a corner on that market," Anton replied. His hand slipped to the small of her back as they stepped into the building, and Grace looked away, knowing she blushed from that small touch alone.

"That's good, that's good." If she kept it short then maybe he wouldn't notice the tremor in her voice. It wasn't from the gentle pressure of Anton's hand on her, but from the thought that maybe, just maybe, the labs would be fine without her constant presence.

She frowned at the unbidden thought, but the hostess arrived, a pretty blonde who was all smiles as she ushered them to a table overlooking the Rhone River.

After they were seated, Anton leaned back in his chair and considered Grace for a moment as she took in the view and sipped from the coffee their server had just set in front of them.

"It's beautiful," she breathed, dark eyes on the river and the view of Mont Blanc in the distance. "Do you come here often?"

"This is my favorite place to come to because of the view."

"Thank you for bringing me." Grace smiled at him over her coffee cup.

"You deserved a little break from the labs after last night."

"They were unholy terrors." She squeezed her eyes shut and gave a little shake of her head. "I am so sorry about everything last night."

"What do you have to be sorry for?"

"Um, them blowing up the bonfire, for one." She laughed and sat back in her chair. "I should have been there making sure it went smooth. And then I was basically Patton when it came to discipline."

"Eh, they deserved it." Anton lifted a shoulder. "You can't be held accountable for what they choose to do though. They are adults."

"Yes, but they are my adults," she countered. "And besides, they are so science-addled and barely exist outside the walls of the lab, so can they really be held accountable for being such wild cards?"

Anton snorted. "Yes, they can."

Grace looked dubious, but said nothing and sipped at her coffee. If what Anton said was true, then would they need her? That was her bit, her contribution to Lou being a science icon. She wrangled. She ensured they ate, drank, refrained from blowing up things, and kept their shrink rays purely theoretical.

What happened if the labs managed to run just fine without her and with Mindy standing in?

What did that mean for her place in the labs if her job could be performed by a stand-in, and all on a day when decaf had been dispersed, for heaven's sake?

Grace picked up her phone and checked her messages, and while she told herself she did it just out of habit a very large part of her hoped there might be a message or two from Lou declaring a state of emergency and begging her to return, but there were none.

She frowned at her empty inbox when Anton reached out and touched her hand.

"What's with the long face?" he asked, fingers gentle on the inside of her wrist.

"Nothing, nothing." She smiled and pushed her hair away from her face. "I'm sorry, I shouldn't—" She gestured to her phone with a grimace. "I'm not usually like this. I'm being rude."

"They'll be fine. I promise."

That was the problem.

Grace sucked in a fortifying breath. "I know you're right. Of course they will be fine," she said with a too-bright smile, and jammed her phone into her bag.

Just then their waiter arrived, and she forced all thoughts of a lab running smoothly without her out of her head. She was on a date with Anton—a brunch no less, complete with a beautiful backdrop, quality coffee, and the promise of breakfast carbs—but somehow her mind was twenty minutes away in her labs wondering if Elisha had passed out yet or if Lou had managed to sneak anything past Mindy.

What was her ever-lovin' problem?

Maybe everything was just a touch too perfect, which was just insane. She should be rejoicing and offering a sacrifice to celebrate the fact that she hadn't been called back to the office. Not moping like a prepubescent teen.

Blowing out a sigh, she fiddled with her coffee cup and raised her eyes to see Anton giving her an assessing look.

It seemed like he could see right through her facade of calm, like he and his stupidly pretty brown eyes could see exactly what was in Grace's mind.

Shifting her eyes to the side, she scrambled to pull their brunch back on track and away from the edge of the rails it threatened to go careening straight off of.

"So what are your plans for the rest of the day?" she tried.

"I had planned on keeping you away from the labs, but I'm seeing now that might not be such a good idea."

"What do you mean, not a good idea?"

Anton steepled his hands and leaned back in his chair. "You're worried about what's going on back there."

"I am not. I mean, okay, I am, but it's just that—"

"Mindy has it under control. I promise."

"But there's a lot to do, and Lou's been faking her naps, which means not good things."

"Trust me. Mindy is more than capable of forcing Lou to rest and keeping the rest of the team in line. It's not like she's never handled an office before. I'm sure there's someone around who can lend a hand if something comes up."

Grace flinched like she'd been slapped.

She knew in her head that Anton hadn't meant to be dismissive. To make it sound like anyone could fill her place. To some, her place at Lou's side wasn't much, but it was *hers*. Finding where she belonged had been the first thing to make her realize just how much damage her upbringing had inflicted on her.

"I know that. You've made it abundantly clear that

Mindy can do my job just fine." Grace raised her menu with a snap of her shaking hands.

"Grace." Anton's voice was gentle, so gentle that Grace knew he'd seen right through her.

"Do you know if the crepes here are good, or should I just go full-on European and get what looks like a world tour of cheese and bread? Or do you want to order something we can share? It would be just *insufferable* if we ate off a shared plate."

"You're not replaceable."

She squeezed her eyes shut, grateful for the semblance of privacy the menu provided.

"Who said that?" she asked, lowering her menu a fraction so she could see over the top at Anton, who still looked at her in far too earnest a manner for what was supposed to be a carefree brunch date.

"You did," he told her, finally looking away from her to pick up his coffee cup.

"Did not."

"Did so."

Grace jutted out her bottom lip. "If I remember correctly, I asked about the state of crepes in this fine establishment. Although I'm considering the wine list to be more handy at the moment."

"If crepes and wine are on your brain, then why are you hoping things go sideways at the lab?"

She blushed and folded her hands in her lap, doing her best to project her best impersonation of a reasonable and well-rounded woman who most certainly did not wish for explosions and science catastrophes.

"I am not hoping things go sideways at the labs. I want there to be nothing but calm and serenity in those walls."

Anton turned his dark eyes back to meet hers. "But when you're there to see it happen."

"Who doesn't like to see a job well done?" she fired back, eyes falling to her menu. She was just going to get wine at the rate this conversation was going.

"Grace, just because Mindy can wrangle science folk doesn't mean that she could ever replace you."

"I never said anything about being replaced," she murmured, flipping the pages of her menu in search of the wine list. To hell with it, she was getting a glass of red.

He folded his hands. "Give me more credit. You're like an open book. It's all over your face."

"I am not an open book, okay? I am a very complicated codex, created by the Mayans and yet to be understood by the Western world," she retorted with her best game face.

"I wouldn't go that far." Anton's hand came to rest in the middle of the wine list she had been staring at. "You wear your heart on your sleeve."

"What's wrong with that?" she asked, finally looking up to meet Anton's gaze. Even as she asked it she knew the answer. What her mother had seen as weakness in her.

Toughen up now, or the world will do it for you.

Anton's voice snapped her out of her second brooding power hour.

"Nothing, but that means I can see what's bothering you, and I'm telling you. Just because the labs don't descend into chaos doesn't mean that you aren't needed. No one is replacing you. That team needs you."

"I'm not a science genius like everyone else," she admitted quietly.

"So?"

"So that means that sometimes I feel like an appendix."

He raised an eyebrow. "A what?"

"An appendix, Anton! Do you know how disheartening it is to feel like the appendix of the group?"

It had been exactly what she'd felt like, upon leaving home for college to discover that her family kept moving along without her, perhaps even better without her under the same roof.

"No?" Anton cautioned with a puzzled look on his face.

"I'll tell you what it feels like. It sucks. That the group you love so much can just keep truckin' without you, so long as there's someone to slap their hands and tell them no. I hate being the appendix, because you can take that thing out and the human body just keeps be-bopping along."

"You are not an appendix."

"Am too," Grace muttered, giving the menu a dark look. "Mindy is managing the labs just fine and I'm here word-vomiting all over you on what should be our very first and very magical brunch date. This is just not the way I thought this would go."

"Life rarely goes that way." He leaned over and caught her hand in his. "But you're not some unnecessary organ prone to inflammation and failure. I knew that the first time I saw you."

"The first time you saw me you called me a food

delivery girl," she reminded him, though she placed her other hand on his.

He grimaced. "I did, but in my defense I was hungover and self-destructive. How about I knew it the first time you made me laugh out loud via email in a board meeting I was supposed to be paying attention in? Or maybe I knew it the first time I heard your voice. Besides, the first time I saw you, I saw a beautiful, confident woman who managed to keep everyone sane. And the next day I saw more of that, and I knew I wanted to be close to it—to *you*. All of the emails, the pining, the random phone calls I prayed didn't look stalkerish—all of it made sense to me because you are the heart, not the appendix of that place. They need someone like you, because otherwise there's no warmth, no caring. It isn't a family without you."

"But you said they were adults and could take care of themselves," Grace whispered.

"That's because I want my girlfriend here with me," Anton replied, raising her hand to his lips. He pressed a kiss to her knuckles and smiled at her. "That comment was motivated by selfish need."

"Oh," Grace breathed. Maybe the labs could wait a few hours, especially if there were more kisses like the one he had just given her.

It was on her hand, for crying out loud! She swallowed hard and leaned toward him.

"What was that about keeping me out of the labs for the day?"

Anton's eyes lit up. "Are you game for playing hooky?"

She licked her lips at the thought of spending the day with Anton and gave his hand a squeeze. You didn't get told a man pined for you by way of emails and not get inspired to play hooky. "Let's do it. It's just one day," she said, giving in to her urge to ignore everything but the man in front of her.

The man who declared she was a heart and not an appendix.

"Right. Everything will be in tip-top shape when we get back." Anton tucked a lock of her hair behind her ear, his foot moving to nudge hers in a gesture that set her heart beating at the speed of light. She swallowed hard, moved her foot against his ankle, and enjoyed the look it put on Anton's face.

"I mean, how much trouble can they really get into?" she mused.

Six hours later...

"They are insane! Little beasts. All of them!" Mindy waved her tablet at the lab behind her.

"But what—"

"What the hell is Lab War?" Mindy barked, shaking what looked to be glitter out of her hair.

Grace's mouth dropped. "Did you just say Lab War?"

When she had wondered how bad things could be she hadn't expected to receive her answer in spades.

Lab War, indeed!

"Yes," Mindy wailed. "One of them made a glitter bomb—I think that's what it was supposed to be? But the glitter keeps multiplying." She shook her blazer and stomped her foot as a fresh wave of glitter cascaded to the floor. "It's like tribbles around here. I don't understand it. I had a cleaning crew in here for two hours."

Grace's eyebrow twitched. "When did the mayhem start?"

"As soon as Elisha fell asleep," Lou muttered, coming to stand beside them. She was also covered in a sheen of glitter, which made her look like an angry pixie. "You were right, by the way; she was out way before lunch."

"And she didn't do this?"

"No, apparently the science horde become monsters when there's no central authority. Just like cartels," Mindy replied, still trying to get glitter off of herself.

"What else happened?"

Lou blinked and rubbed her eyes. "I don't know. I fell asleep."

"Good, you slept at least." Grace breathed a sigh of relief. "This could have been worse if you and Elisha weren't knocked out."

"Worse?" Mindy raised an eyebrow. "How could that even be possible? I caught one of them trying to create a new adhesive they were hell-bent on using on my team. Plus there's the fact that I have no idea what to even feed them. It's like having an army of sleepy toddlers running rampant. How do none of them take a lunch or know how to feed themselves? I have no idea how you do this." She shook her head and stepped closer to Anton, who leaned against the doorway.

"I'm not looking so bad now, am I?" he asked with a smirk.

"I will never ever berate your poor health habits again. You're practically well-rounded and well-adjusted in comparison."

"Gee, that gets me right in the ticker." Anton clutched a hand to his chest. "I missed you too, dear."

Mindy said nothing, but went to Anton and rested her forehead on his shoulder.

"Never leave me again," she ordered.

Anton patted her head. "Wouldn't dream of it."

"It couldn't have been that bad." Grace shook her head and stepped further into the labs, her eyes scanning the scene to see a group of recalcitrant scientists staring death glares at one another. The room was split down the middle with Anton's group on one side and hers on the other. A snoring Elisha worked at the line of demarcation between the two, and Grace rolled her eyes, striding forward into the tense room.

"Can anyone tell me why you've decided to declare a civil war in here?" she asked, looking around. "You're all professionals. This should be the time you all come together and learn from each other, not descend to glitter bomb fights."

"Tell that to them," Karen, one of Lou's team leaders, said, pointing a finger across the room. "They walked in here acting like they owned the place."

"That's a lie," one of Anton's scientists fired back. "You're all too busy acting like we don't belong. You won't even share the coffee."

"That's because it was decaf," Karen yelled. "If you think I'm going to share what little caffeine I've been allocated, then you're mistaken. We're on war rations, and that means everyone for themselves, okay?"

"It's your fault we even had to put up with decaf," another New York scientist barked out. "Why were you trying to set us on fire?"

"Because your boss was getting handsy with our lab lady. We aren't letting her go down like that," another physicist to Grace's right piped up, prompting a chorus of agreement from the lab team. She stopped short when she realized what she was hearing.

She swallowed hard, blinking back the tears that threatened to spill from her eyes, "Wait, are you telling me that you've been acting out to defend my honor?"

"Of course! Why else do you think Elisha would risk decaffeination?" Karen said, jabbing a finger at Elisha, still facedown on the lab table in front of her. "I mean, look at her. She's in a puddle of her own drool. She did that for you."

"I overcaffeinated her," Grace admitted. She still reeled from the fact that her lab team had exploded a bonfire and let loose a glitter plague for the sake of her honor.

A fire was one thing, but glitter?

Glitter was forever. Glitter meant business.

Glitter was love.

Grace sniffled at the gesture. "I'm really—I don't know what to say to you all. That was really sweet."

A murmur went up through the crowd, and Karen shook her head. "You're a scary lab queen, Grace, but you're our scary lab queen, and we've heard all about Kovalev." She leveled a steely look over Grace's shoulder at the man in question, who sauntered up beside Grace with an easy smile.

"Your dedication to defending your sovereign. is admirable, but I assure you, I've only got the best intentions at heart when it comes to Grace." He slipped his hand into hers and tugged her close.

"Is that so?" Karen crossed her arms, and Grace could tell from the set of her shoulders visions of her next lab-fueled prank danced through her mind like deranged sugar plums.

Grace loved her minions so very, very much.

"It is. In fact, she's made a semi-honest man of me," Anton replied, turning and giving the room the same smile that Grace could imagine on the covers of newspapers and gossip rags alike. The man was in full charming mode, and from the softening look on Karen and the gathered team's faces, Grace could tell it was working.

"What's that mean?" another physicist asked.

"It means we are dating," he said with another thousand-watt smile. "I even took her to brunch and let her shop for antiques. It's all on the up-and-up."

Karen's mouth dropped open, and a particularly loud snore by Elisha punctuated the shock that rippled through both teams.

"Really? That's what the bouquet was about?" Karen pressed. Grace nodded and leaned into Anton's side.

"Don't worry, I'm not a fallen woman—at least not yet." She tapped her chin. "But, like, what's actually wrong with being a fallen woman? It seems fun." She shook her head when she saw Karen tilt her head in confusion, and focused on getting the science horde to back down. "But if you could all keep this quiet, well, I'd appreciate it."

"We'll be good, for now," Karen huffed before turning her eyes on Anton. "But if you hurt her, we will rain holy terror on you and yours."

A murmur of agreement went up from Grace's team, which made her simultaneously want to roll her eyes in annoyance and hug each and every one of them within an inch of their lives.

She would end the caffeine embargo immediately, *and* bake them cookies.

Anton dipped his head in acknowledgment. "I wouldn't expect anything less."

"Get back to work," Grace sighed. "But thank you. It just means a lot that you had my back. You all get cookies tomorrow." A cheer went up from the group—even Anton's lab rats joined in—and Grace turned away, a smile tugging at her lips.

"Just an appendix, hmm?" he asked, dark eyes dancing at the blush that swept over her cheeks.

"No one likes a gloater, Mr. Kovalev," she whispered to him.

CHAPTER EIGHT

"It's the great tragedy - people employed in ways that don't fully tap everything they do best in life."
—Neil deGrasse Tyson

"Where's Grace?" Anton blinked, looking around the lab —which looked utterly sideways. That morning, Grace had kept up a steady stream of flirty texts, some of them even downright scandalous.

Just the way Anton liked them.

But then Grace had gone radio silent. Silence wasn't something Grace did often, and it concerned him.

Anton had pulled himself away from fine-tuning the new batch of lenses he'd had shipped in from New York months ago. Normally, he would oversee the work on the telescope via teleconference or detailed notes, but now that he was here the opportunity to do the work himself was too tempting to pass up.

There had been the problem of overcoming Geneva's

less-than-suitable altitude for infrared tech. Higher was better for infrared telescopes, and the paltry 1,200-foot elevation of Geneva was unfit for what Lou's research demanded. Unable to change her research appointment location, Anton had devised a way to make up for the limited elevation. RED's specifications, for use in a variety of elevations and conditions, was just the thing they needed to make this work.

He lived for this. Taking apart a problem and fitting it back together after he'd perfected it made his blood sing, but he suspected that might be what anyone would encounter when making something capable of glimpsing the farthest reaches of the universe. It was like the sci-fi novels he'd read brought to life and so much bigger than anything on earth.

The stars had been one of the main reasons for him cleaning up his act. They'd always been there, shining through each and every one of his fuck-ups. Anton had set them as his course to a better version of himself, for a life that meant more than just partying and fleeting pleasure.

And yet...even with his team around him and the lens fittings going well, that familiar feeling of excitement at seeing a project come together was overshadowed by Grace's absence.

What was the world really coming to, if this was the state of affairs?

Of course, ensuring that Beta's final retrofit was complete was of the utmost importance, but...then there was Grace. You didn't just send the string of emojis she had sent to him and then disappear.

Aside from that, Anton Kovalev wasn't used to women going silent. And especially not when he was their boyfriend, which prompted him to give everyone an early lunch on the pretense of seeing if Grace would like to join him. His feet had brought him to the one place he knew Grace would be. But upon seeing the disarray, Anton wondered if he'd guessed wrong.

It looked like she hadn't set foot in the labs in a month, let alone that morning. Something very, very wrong had happened.

"Where's Grace?" he tried again, and sidestepped a puddle of unknown substance.

"I don't know," Elisha barked, stomping past him with a pinched look on her face. "Not here." She jabbed a finger at the lab behind her, where a couple of interns scrambled to pick up a stack of fallen papers from the floor.

He sniffed the air. "Is something burning?"

"I had nothing to do with any of this," Elisha muttered, backing away from him.

"Any of what?" Anton asked.

A resounding bang made them both jump, and Elisha looked around with wide eyes.

"That." She waved a hand behind her. "All of that. Grace isn't here, which means Lou is running rampant, okay? And that's bad. It's like the science horde are a hive mind and they're just feeding off of her science mania."

"Alrighty then," Anton called after Elisha when she turned on her heel and bolted for the doors. If the woman who had exploded a whole bonfire would have none of the Geneva labs, then Anton wasn't sure how he felt about pushing his own luck.

Cautioning another look around the lab, he pushed on, careful to avoid a pile of what looked to be orange slime. Traces of glitter could be seen gleaming from desks here and there.

"It won't damage the equipment—these science freaks made sure of it—but god, it's annoying," Grace had said with a glare the previous day.

Running a finger along a desk, Anton hummed at the glittery residue that came away on his finger. There was a certain charm to the whole thing. Even with the scientists acting as if they were wild boxcar hobos.

"Curiouser and curiouser," he murmured, still picking his way through the lab. There were fast food containers across one set of tables, an overturned pair of stools, and even a half-empty bottle of vodka sitting on the floor.

What the hell had gone on here?

And what was Lou up to? Anton tilted his head, trying to catch a sound from the woman, but heard nothing in the immediate area. She wasn't in the labs—at least not the immediate area—but she was close by... But that still didn't explain Grace's absence, or the state of her usually orderly and pristine labs.

"Has anyone seen Grace?" Anton tried. The remnants of the physicists shook their heads.

"We aren't supposed to—" one of them began, before they received an elbow from their counterpart.

"Shut it!"

Anton snapped his fingers at them. "Hey—shut it? Pray tell, why?" When the pair of scientists looked like they might bolt, Anton glared at them. "I sign the checks around here, so if you know what's good for you, you'll sing like a canary."

They both made a face at Anton's threat. "Crap," one of them muttered.

"Exactly. Now sing," Anton ordered, coming to stand beside them.

"Lou is on a science bender," one said with a nervous look over their shoulder.

"And?" Anton prompted.

"Grace got sick and Lou just…" They shook their head and then waved their fingers. "It was like she just sort of took off into outer space. And there's no one to stop her."

"I heard she fakes her naps," the other scientist added.

"Wait, Grace is sick?" Anton stood up straighter and peered around the lab with new eyes. Everything was beginning to click into place.

"This morning she went down like a ton of bricks."

"Where is she?" Anton whirled around, scanning the lab for Grace's bright pink hair.

"I'd check by her desk," one of them supplied with a knowing look. "That's all I'm going to say."

"But there's no one over there." Anton cautioned a look toward the desk, before he pushed away from the two scientists. When he stood next to the desk, he spied what looked to be a sneaker sticking out from beneath the desk.

"Grace?" he tried.

A groan answered him and he sighed, stepping around the desk to see Grace huddled under her desk, glassy-eyed, with a mug of steaming chicken noodle soup to her nose. Scattered among the tissues were what looked to be an assortment of sharpies, a few random work papers, and a bottle of cough syrup. Anton clucked his tongue when he glimpsed the shiny metal of an emergency blanket wrapped around her shivering shoulders.

Grace wasn't just sick.

The woman needed to be in quarantine.

"What are you doing down here?" Anton asked, squatting down in front of her.

Grace blinked at him and sniffled. "I'm just, you know…around." She shifted to the side, the crinkling emergency blanket fluttering around her.

"Around?" Anton shook his head, eyes tracking the silver blanket's movements. "I think you mean sick."

Her brown eyes widened. "No. I'm not sick. That's crazy. I have way too much work to be sick." She scrambled around, fingers reaching for papers she thrust at Anton. He bit back a sigh when he saw they were nothing more than a few half hearted equations scribbled across manila folders. A tissue hung from one of them.

Anton sighed. "You're sick."

"That's propaganda."

"You're wearing an emergency blanket like a cape."

"Kiss me, hot stuff." She puckered her lips at him, to which Anton jerked back and made a cross symbol at her.

"Get your germs out of here," he ordered with a stern look.

Giving up her femme fatale angle, Grace sighed. "How'd you find me anyway?" she asked, narrowing her eyes at him. "I'm not sick. Who put you up to this? Elisha?"

"Last I saw of her, she was running for the veritable hills."

Grace took a deep inhale of steam from her soup. "The hills? Good riddance, I say."

"Come out from under there, Grace. We need to get you home."

Grace shied away from him with a frown. "This is my home."

"When was the last time you slept?"

"Sleep is for the weak of will."

Anton scrubbed a hand over his face and made a grab for her, but Grace only scuttled further away from him until her back hit the rear of her desk.

"Hands off, pretty boy," she said, shoving her pink hair out of her face with a frown.

"That's it." Anton reached out a hand and caught Grace around the ankle. "You're coming out of there one way..." He tugged and Grace yelped when she slid forward. "Or another."

"Unhand me, you cad," Grace yelled, throwing a handful of sharpies his way. "You absolute beast!"

"Yeah, uh huh, heard it all before," Anton grunted, dodging a manila folder as he hooked his other hand around Grace's thighs and yanked her toward him. In Anton's opinion, women were unruly as a whole, and he had no idea how to handle them when they were healthy, much less when they were sick. Grace, fighting to stay under her desk when all he wanted to do was get her home and to a doctor, was a prime piece of evidence that the fairer sex could be, at times, completely unreasonable.

That didn't stop him from wanting to take care of the

pink-haired woman, no matter how many sharpies she hurled a him.

He had it bad.

Shaking his head at himself, Anton hauled Grace out from under the desk. Only when he stood, arms holding Grace against him, did she go dramatically limp in his hold.

"You're like Rhett Butler," she murmured, head lolling against his shoulder. Her glazed eyes fixed on his face, and she gave him a dreamy smile.

"Are you swooning?" Anton shifted her to the desk in front of them and held a hand against her forehead. Her skin was hot to the touch, and he shook his head. "You've definitely got a fever, so it's either you're swooning or you're delirious and in danger of fainting."

"Aren't they both kind of the same?" she asked, still cradling her soup mug against her chest.

Anton pursed his lips. "You know what? They are. But that doesn't change the fact that you're sick." He scooped her back up into his arms and tried to ignore the happy little sigh that escaped Grace's lips as he carried her through the labs.

"Where are we going?"

"There's a medical office here. I'm getting you meds and then taking you home and putting you to bed."

"How scandalous." Grace waved her soup mug. "I approve."

"Not that kind of bed, you little monster."

"Me? I'm an angel—an angel that isn't sick!" She kicked her feet and glared at him. "I have a lab to manage.

Not one but two teams to keep an eye on. You can't just take me from my work, okay?"

Anton remained unfazed. "Too bad. You're sick. You're going home."

"This is a dirty smear campaign. Put me down. I've got a science horde to wrangle. If I don't get them in hand, then they could explode something—maybe each other. Lou has probably already set her sights on the moon, Anton. We have to go back."

"In case you haven't noticed, this place has already gone down a very Mad Max road, and it can stay that way for all I care." Anton slowed as he came to the lab doors, and turned once more to survey the carnage left in the wake of Grace's absence.

Grace blinked hazy eyes at him. "What? Mad Max? You mean Lou has taken over already?"

"Completely. But that's for another time." Anton kicked the door of the lab open and ignored the starry-eyed look Grace sent up at him from under her lashes. The woman had the ability to look sexy in any circumstance, even when she had a tissue hanging from her nose and her hair was in disarray.

"I take it back. You're not Rhett, you're a—you're a Viking."

"Is that so?" Anton asked, striding down the hall, eyes moving along the signs directing him toward the medical office.

Grace hummed. "You bet your tight and toned ass." She swung her legs from her perch in Anton's arms. "You go the gym, don't you? I mean, like what? Three or twelve times a week?"

"Stop trying to butter me up," he replied. "I'm not letting you go back to the lab."

She stuck out her lip. "You're a real thorn in a lab queen's side, Kovalev."

~

GRACE GLARED UP AT HIM.

She wasn't happy, but she was sick, so that meant Anton didn't care. He hadn't signed up to be someone's boyfriend just to let them run wild and rampant in the streets with a fever of 104 degrees. He may not be skilled in the relationship department, but he was sure letting a significant other wilfully endanger their health for the sake of science was a no-no in *The Big Book of How to Care for Your Girlfriend.*

Anton never did anything by half measures, and that meant he was going to take care of Grace. No matter how much she whined.

And the woman was an Olympic whiner.

"Stop trying to give me murder eyes and go to sleep," he ordered, yanking the fluffy comforter over her shoulders.

She crossed her arms over her chest. "I keep telling you. I'm fine. The doctor said so."

"Liar."

She pouted. "They said I wasn't contagious."

"That doesn't mean you're not sick."

Grace glared, but she sank back against the pillows. "You're a tyrant."

"Save the pet names for when we're in bed."

Her cheeks colored in a way unassociated with her fever, and she licked her lips. "I hoped that would be tonight."

Anton groaned and shook his head. "Don't tease. Besides, I'm taking you out all fancy schmancy on a true date. You're not going to be up for that for days."

"But the doctor said it was just a bug. That it could be gone early tomorrow morning, even."

"Then we'll just have to wait and see, won't we?" Anton asked, rocking back on his heels and giving her a stern look.

"Couldn't we plan for a slumber party tomorrow night, then?"

Anton froze in the act of placing a glass of water on her bedside table. "Slumber party?" he asked, even though he already knew what Grace meant.

"Don't get all coy on me now." She winked at him and leaned back on her pillows in what she probably intended to be a suggestive pose, and it would have been if she hadn't immediately erupted into a coughing fit.

"Get some rest, dear." He tossed a tissue box onto the bed beside her.

"Anton, I have to get back into those labs. What does a woman have to do to get her way around here?" She wiped her nose with the back of her hand and looked at him meaningfully, but the sexy spell had already been broken.

"You are going to stay in that bed—alone," he added when she made a swipe for him. "You're going to take your medicine, and I'll check in later tonight."

"Anton, I really am feeling—"

"If the next word out of your mouth is 'better,' I'll lock you out of the labs for another 24 hours."

She gasped. "You wouldn't dare."

"Wouldn't I?" He arched an eyebrow at her. "Now that you're down for the count, it's up to me to keep the science horde in line. Mindy is the auxiliary on this, and I have to go talk Lou down from shooting herself up into the cosmos. Now get some rest."

"Make sure that you give her orange slices once she's back to normal. Going all science overlord makes her dehydrated," Grace called after him.

Anton waved his hand in acknowledgment but kept his feet moving toward the door. Once he locked up and got on his way back to the labs, he dug out his phone and fired off a quick text to Mindy.

"On my way back. What's the situation?"

Almost immediately a text pinged through his phone.

"Lou wore herself out. We got lucky."

"Jesus," Anton breathed, shoulders sinking in relief. He'd anticipated having to bribe the woman down with the promise of unlimited funding and no supervision, but this made things easy.

He was just about to climb into his car when he paused. When he had left it hadn't seemed like Lou was in danger of slowing down—but now she had worn herself out? He bit his lip and wondered how that happened.

"Best not to ask," Anton murmured, shifting the car into drive. If Mindy had managed it, then Mindy had managed it, and the less he knew the less culpable he would be when Grace and apparently Lou regained their faculties.

And if Anton were honest, he'd much rather be on the nice list than the revenge list when Grace recovered, because there was the matter of the slumber party. The entire drive back to the lab, Anton's mind strayed close to the idea of a healthy and beguiling Grace, so much so that he had to give himself a firm pep talk about the importance of driving safety.

Thankfully, he arrived back at the labs without incident, and was able to witness the tail end of Lou's science bender.

Mindy stood, tablet in hand and a glare on her face. "Move it. All of you," she snapped at the group of scientists shuffling forward, their heads hanging and shoulders drooping.

Anton blinked, taking in the defeated-looking group. "What the hell happened here? When I said clean up I didn't mean break their souls."

"In this day and age that's practically the same thing, so be more specific next time." Mindy sighed and put her tablet down on the table. "Besides, that wasn't me. That was Lou."

"Lou? What the hell?" Anton ran a hand through his hair. During his friendship with the woman he'd never thought she had it in her, but she *had* threatened to maim him, so he supposed it was in there somewhere.

"I found them working away like a bunch of serfs. I got Lou to pass out not too long after."

"About that." Anton tilted his head to the side. "How'd you pull off that feat of strength?"

Mindy shrugged and looked away. "Do you really want to know all the sordid details?" she asked, running a hand over her hair. She turned and looked at Anton when he didn't immediately answer. "Be careful, though. You know what they say about curiosity and the cat."

"Christ Almighty." Anton shook his head and stepped back. "All I asked was how you got her to turn down the supervillian act, not if you waterboarded her. What's with all the women around here going rogue? Haven't you all heard of the Geneva Convention?"

Mindy rolled her eyes and snatched up her tablet. "Must you be so dramatic all the time?"

Anton pinched the bridge of his nose between his forefinger and thumb. "Sometimes I swear you just want to drive me to an early grave to get your hands on my will."

Mindy perked up. "Oh. Am I in it? I want the fine china your mother gave you."

"Not anymore you're not. I'm leaving everything to a cat that I have yet to adopt, but it will have one eye and a stench that makes your eyes water. You'll be indebted to him forever. In fact, you're going to have to call him sir."

"You don't even like cats," Mindy said, voice deadpan, but her lips turned up in a smile.

"That's why it's perfect.

"Perfect? And you're really in a tizzy because I said you were dramatic?"

"An unfounded claim."

"Drama king."

Anton sniffed. "You know what? That doesn't have a bad ring to it. At least not the king part."

"Oh god. That's it. I'm leaving. I didn't even get lunch. You know what? You can sort the rest of this mess out."

Mindy stuck her tongue out at him and turned on her heel.

"Get back here, or I'll get two cats."

"Ta." Mindy wiggled her fingers over her shoulder as she breezed through the doors.

"Half tempted to set it on fire and take the loss," he muttered, turning to survey the aftereffects of Lou's reign of science terror.

He sighed, toeing at an empty cup of coffee before he brightened and stood up taller. There was always the option of taking his leave the same way Mindy had escaped. He took a quick step toward the door. If he vanished into the night with the rest of them, then they would all just have to deal with the mess in the morning and—

He almost groaned as a thought came to him with all the force of a freight train.

They wouldn't deal with it.

Grace would. And Grace was sick.

He couldn't leave the labs the way they were for her to deal with. It wasn't right.

The door opened and Anton's head shot up. It was the janitor.

"Thank god it's you. Look." He pointed around him with a few jabs of his fingers. "There's been a situation, but if—"

"I told them I wouldn't clean up another science mess." The janitor jerked back from the door like they had been burned and waved an arm. "Not after last time."

"Last time?" Anton croaked.

"Last time there was a fire."

"There's not a fire this time..."

"Consider yourself lucky, but this isn't on me."

"But I can pay you. Whatever you're making, I'll triple it," Anton said, rushing toward the door, but the janitor would have none of it.

"Not enough. Here's a broom." The janitor launched a broom at him and Anton jumped back, managing to catch it before it smacked him in the face.

"You didn't need to throw it like a javelin. What do you think this is, Sparta?"

The door snapped shut behind the janitor, and Anton sucked his lips against his teeth with a wince.

He tossed his coat on a table and looked at the broom. He'd swept before, so he could do this.

How hard could it be, right? Lou was the size of a mouse. She couldn't have made that much of a mess.

CHAPTER NINE

"In nature nothing exists alone."
—Rachel Carson

"So you're feeling better?" Lou asked.

Grace unwrapped her scarf from around her neck. "Right as rain, boss lady."

Lou balanced the three-tier stack of coffees she carried and nodded. "That's good, that's good, I—well, I'm just happy you're better." The smaller woman kept nodding to herself as they walked down the hallway toward the labs.

"You didn't have to get coffee. I could have done that," Grace said, giving side-eye to the herbal tea Lou had thrust at her when she'd entered the building a few minutes ago.

"You're just saying that because I gave you tea," Lou replied.

Grace pulled a face as she took a sip. "But why tea? I'm

not Bridget Jones, okay? I need coffee and lots of it to function properly."

"I said no."

"You know what? I don't like it when you're being the responsible caretaker one out of us." Grace pouted and took another sip of her tea before she made a face.

"Stop being so dramatic. That is a very nice chamomile tea."

Grace glared at the cup of tea. "That's sleepy-time tea. What are you trying to do to me?"

Lou didn't answer, and when she stopped just short of the lab doors in front of them Grace had to hop to the side to avoid crashing into her. Grace looked up from her cup to see Lou staring at the double doors like she had just realized something.

And from the look of her wide brown eyes, that something wasn't good.

"Oh hell," Lou hissed.

"Lou? What's wrong?"

"I was left unsupervised, okay?" Lou whirled on her friend with a shake of her head. "You know how I get when you're not here."

Grace fell back a step. "Oh no. What did you do?"

"I saw some very compelling data—"

"You went on a science bender, didn't you?!" Grace yelled.

Lou gave the stack of coffees a dangerous shake. "It was just so tempting..."

"Lou, please tell me you didn't set anything on fire. You promised the janitor you wouldn't."

"It wasn't even that big, you know," Lou said.

"I was sick for one day!"

"I know, I know," Lou said, her eyes dropping to the coffees in front of her. "To be fair, I almost waited until lunchtime before I went nuts."

"How self-disciplined of you." Her hands went to her hips and she sucked her lips between her teeth as she stared down the double doors with Lou. Her friend's sudden reluctance to enter the labs now made all the sense in the world.

Who know what crime scene awaited them?

"Come on, let's go see the damage you wrought, you little monster."

"Well, I'm *your* little monster," Lou muttered, trailing behind Grace as she pushed the doors open. "I got you tea."

"But at what cost?" Grace asked, a grimace already on her face when she thought about the work it would take to clean the labs up. "I don't care if my immune system is weakened. I demand coffee. That's the only way I'm going to be able to cl—"

Her rant died on her lips when she turned and took in the labs.

The labs, which weren't a wreck.

The labs that were, in fact, intact and spotless.

A sleeping Anton lay front and center on a table, a cleaning rag still clutched in one hand. She felt her heart clench, chest feeling too tight to breathe.

How long must he have been here, to fall asleep on a table?

She bit her lip and took in a shaky breath, crossing the labs to him.

She had just brushed her knuckles against his cheek when Lou bounded into the room.

"Will you look at that," Lou said with a flourish of her arms. "Exactly how I left them."

"Yeah, uh huh." Grace raised an eyebrow and shook her head at the relieved look on her friend's face. "You think I was born yesterday? I know what you did."

"Where's your proof?"

Grace flicked a finger at Anton. "There's my proof. Don't think I don't know he Cinderella'd this place back into shape."

"I think you mean Sleeping Beauty. Look at the little darling," Lou cooed, leaning over the table to look at Anton, who was—judging by the long-suffering sigh—now awake.

"Let a man sleep," Anton groaned, rolling over and throwing an arm over his eyes. "You're worse than the NYPD in Central Park waking me up. This is America, isn't it? Can't a man just sleep where he wants these days?"

"No," Lou shot back.

"Why not?"

"Because you're in Europe."

"Ugh."

"How long did it take you to clean up Lou's mess?" Grace asked, hands on her hips.

Anton waved his hand and turned over onto his side. "I don't want to talk about it. I thought it would never end." He rubbed his eyes and fixed a bleary gaze on Lou. "How did you manage to make the mess you did? You're so small. I swear to god, the things I found stuck to the ceiling were indescribable."

Lou rolled her eyes and began to unpack the coffee and bagels she had picked up that morning. "You're being dramatic," she told him, handing a container of fruit to Grace when the other woman went to snag a bagel.

"But carbs…" Grace whined.

"You need antioxidants." Lou thrust the fruit into Grace's hands.

"She's right," Anton muttered, pushing himself away from the table and almost tripping over the mop as he went. "Eat the fruit."

"But I had fever dreams of warm carbs. That's what I want."

"I don't have it in me to clean the labs again, which means you are getting rest and vitamins and water and sunlight. You're like a very sexy houseplant that we need to keep alive." He pushed her down into a chair. "Now eat the damn fruit."

"He's right." Lou joined her with a little smile. "We need our Gracie in tip-top health, and besides, I kind of scared myself yesterday with how deep I got with everything."

Grace speared a bit of melon with her fork and groaned. "Please tell me you didn't try to mind meld with anything otherworldly."

Lou laughed. "I didn't." She paused and then blinked. "I mean, I don't think—wait a second…"

"I'm going to pretend that you didn't just look unsure about that," Grace said as she sipped another mouthful of watery tea. She sniffed the air with a barely restrained moan of frustration.

It wasn't right. She hadn't risen like Lazarus only to be

force-fed fruit and tea when the smell of coffee and carbs was heavy in the air.

"You're bullies, the both of you," she accused, jabbing a grape so hard it split in two.

Anton came to stand beside her with a yawn. "Oh yes, because we want to take care of you, the horror of it all," he deadpanned before dropping a kiss on her head. "Eat your fruit and stuff it, sweetheart."

Grace flushed at the casual touch and endearment.

"Thank you," she said, catching his hand when he moved to step away. "For everything, for just—you didn't have to put the labs back together again for me."

"No problem." He winked at her and then surprised her when he moved close, fingers warm on her hand as he raised her hand to his lips. "No problem at all for you." His breath was warm on her skin and a second later he brushed his lips against her knuckles, once, twice, and then finally a third time.

"Oh, her lady bits like that," Lou crowed as she handed out coffees to the physicists who had begun a wary shuffle into the labs.

Grace's eyes squeezed shut in exasperation. "Shut your adorable face, Lou."

"Well, I can tell, you know."

Grace's cheeks flushed bright red at Lou's peanut gallery comments. While Anton laughed, he hadn't let go of her hand. His breath came out warm and soft over her skin, making her fingertips itch with anticipation over what it might feel like to have her hands on his body without so many clothes involved.

"Lady bits," Lou sang as she breezed by with a coffee in each hand.

"I'm going to murder her," Grace said.

Anton's eyes dropped from her hand to her mouth. "I, for one, am interested in the accuracy of the information she's proclaiming."

"Oh."

He nodded at her, dark eyes moving in a slow lazy path down her neck and chest. "Oh," he agreed, reaching out to rest a hand against her hip. "Now, I seem to remember talk of a slumber party when you were feeling better."

"That's right." She licked her lips, leaning into his touch with a sigh.

"Tonight?" he asked, lifting a hand to tuck her hair behind her ear. His fingers skimmed down along the curve of her jaw. "After I get a nap, but tonight?"

Grace's lips parted against the brush of his thumb. How had her life gotten to this place? "Y-yes," she stammered out, head swimming from his proximity. She was still floored by the fact that he had labored into the night to clean up Lou's science madness, and all for her. "You're a top-notch boyfriend, Kovalev."

"I know." He gave her a smile as he raised his other hand up to cup her face, and Grace forgot how to breathe. When he tilted her head back, fingers gentle but firm, she straight-up forgot how to think.

Blessedly, she didn't need her brain for what came next.

Her eyes drifted closed and Anton leaned into her, his lips claiming hers in a long overdue kiss.

She snaked her arms around his neck when she felt the brush of his tongue against her bottom lip. Her lips parted, and one of Anton's hands moved to her hip, pulling her flush against him as he backed her into the table behind her, prompting a moan that most definitely told everyone within earshot that she was the type of woman to not only entertain lewd thoughts in public, but had the fortitude to act upon said thoughts.

Public.

Oh, right.

Grace forced herself to stop, and though she hated every second of it she untangled herself from Anton with a shaky breath. When they stood a safe distance from one another, she gave him an accusing look.

"I thought you weren't good at this relationship stuff," she whisper-screamed at him. "You bamboozled me."

Anton shook his head and held out his hands. "I didn't know. Besides, it's not as hard as I thought it wou—"

"They stole it," Elisha's voice rang through the labs, causing Grace and Anton to spring back from one another in surprise.

Lou paused in the act of double-fisting her coffee and looking over that morning's reports.

"What do you mean?" Grace breathed, though she had a sinking feeling she knew exactly what Elisha would say.

"I mean that our latest data is gone. Every last byte of it has been wiped from the servers. We've been robbed."

~

THERE WAS nothing quite like the feeling of someone

coming in to your home and taking your nearest and dearest possessions to put a damper on a lady boner.

Grace frowned at the computer screen in front of her. She had been staring at it with unseeing eyes for the past fifteen minutes under the guise of helping fix the mess they were in, except that she didn't have the slightest ghost of a baby angel's prayer of knowing where to begin in trying to "fix" anything.

She glanced up over her computer monitor to see Lou pacing and staring at the floor as she muttered to herself. Understandably, the scientist was in shock.

Elisha had been correct in her assessment that they had been robbed.

At precisely 4:06 that morning, someone had swiped into the area that all of their unanalyzed data lived in. It was a room that required a high security clearance card, of which there were only four.

And of those four, one of them was in Grace's possession.

She reached into her jacket pocket and fingered the slim plastic keycard to reassure herself that she hadn't dropped it somewhere in the hallways of CERN for some thieving vagabond to swipe and use to wreak absolute havoc on her life.

She pursed her lips in thought. Though she was certain the building had never even seen the shadow of a vagabond, it didn't stop her from being sure only someone outside of their team could have been responsible for such a gutting loss.

The research that had been stolen had taken the better part of six months to complete. They had been collecting it since they had set up in the labs. Lou was destroyed over the loss, not so much because of the data but because of the time spent.

Time was the irreplaceable resource that Lou swore she was in a losing battle with. It took no less than three weeks to observe a pulsar wave—or, rather, the pulsar timing array that clued them in to the neutron star's behavior. Some pulsar timing arrays had been in observation for decades and had proved more or less predictable. The ones Lou had her research sights set on were newly discovered, very young pulsars acting out of character for newly formed neutron stars. Their paths to either black holes or supernovae were still to be determined. Yet the energy outputs made no sense.

Every scientist on Lou's team knew just how much the data sets they had spent weeks collecting meant to their end goal.

With every unpredictable behavior from pulsar waves and the uncertainty of observing the same exact output from the neutron stars more than once, the data was priceless.

And now it was gone.

A sniffle from Lou's direction made Grace's hands curl into fists.

"What's with the look on your face?" Anton nodded at her and set a cup of coffee in front of her.

"Oh, this?" Grace indicated her face with a finger. "This is just my 'getting ready to murder thieves' face."

"Murder?"

Grace punched a fist into her palm and narrowed her eyes. "They made my best friend cry. They're lucky murder is all I'm going to do when I get my hands on them."

Anton opened his mouth to speak, but paused and tilted his head to the side as he considered her threat. "But isn't murder the extreme of things you could do?"

"Yeah, if I lacked imagination. But I don't, which means they would be lucky."

"What is it with the women in this lab? You're all absolutely terrifying." Anton gave Grace a quick look of reproach, but she only shot him a wink.

"And don't you forget it, Kovalev," she said, and blew him an air kiss.

Anton's hand shot out and caught said kiss, and brought it close to his chest. His hand had moved as if on autopilot. He blinked and stared wide-eyed at the hand pressed against his heart. "I don't know what it says about me that I'm here for this. I'm not okay with who you're turning me into."

She shrugged. "What can I say? You're a modern man who knows what he's about. Even if you insist on fighting it. Now follow me, because I've got a plan to catch this thief."

"A plan?" Anton pushed away from the table and followed behind Grace, who began walking at a speed considered respectable in professional power-walking circles.

"No, not a plan." She stopped short, nearly causing Anton to careen into her. He leapt to the side with a yelp, but Grace didn't notice as she whirled around, pink hair flying out around her, and gave him a serious look. "This is so much bigger than a plan. Why are you plastered to the wall?"

Anton rolled his eyes and leaned back against the wall where he had landed. "So what is it?" he dared to ask, feeling more sure on his feet.

"A caper."

"Pardon?"

"A *caper,*" Grace repeated, putting emphasis on the key word. A well-executed caper could do wonders for even the smallest of mysteries, let alone catching the thief who had broken Lou's heart.

Anton pushed away from the wall. "Saying it again isn't going to make me understand," he told her.

She gave him an incredulous look. "Were you raised by wolves, Kovalev? Everyone in the know is hip to what a caper entails."

"I missed the memo. Enlighten me."

"A caper. An adventure chock-full of hijinks, stakeouts, and witty banter." She stopped and wagged a finger. "And smooching. Lots of smooching, because we deserve to live our best lives even when we're in pursuit of horrible people."

Anton smiled at her and leaned forward in his seat, elbows braced on the desk in front of him. "Now I can get behind a plan that promises smooching. But what does this caper business entail?"

Grace pulled him down the hallway. "A caper is just the thing to get our relationship off to a solid start," she said with the air of someone in the know.

"Nothing more official than a bit of thief nabbing to

really solidify a new relationship, eh?" Anton smiled at her in agreement, making Grace's breath catch.

"I agree," she said. "Just the thing to make it official." She opened the door to her office, a rarely used space as it didn't allow her to keep an eye on restless scientists with a penchant for recklessness, and ushered him inside.

Lou was already there, hands on her hips, staring at what Grace considered one of her finer creations. After having the data stolen, Grace may have gone on a science bender of her own, compiling a list of names for the lab teams, another list of possible motives, swipe card times she had retrieved from the surveillance server, and a tentative timeline for the theft.

As a visual learner, Grace had raided their supply closet for the colored tape and created a web that would have done any primetime mystery show proud. It was a masterpiece of detective work. A masterpiece of investigation. A veritable vision of Sherlockian skill. A marvel. It was—

"What the hell is this?" Lou asked, jerking her head at the board.

"That," Grace said, flouncing into the room, "is how we are going to catch a thief."

CHAPTER TEN

"Be less curious about people and more curious about ideas."
—Marie Curie

"What...what exactly are we looking at?" Anton asked, leaning back in his chair. They had retreated to a coffee shop following a detailed explanation from Grace on the board in all its intricate details. But instead of coffee and conversation with his new girlfriend, Grace had made a beeline for a window booth and had been studying the sidewalk outside of the window with the focus of a zen master.

"And why are you wearing that ridiculous hat?" He nodded at the oversized yellow beanie with a large knitted daisy perched on top. It looked like what would happen if a Cabbage Patch Kid managed to drag itself from the field and come of age.

Grace's eyes slid to his, and she let out a beleaguered sigh. "It's called fashion, honey. Look it up."

Anton rolled his eyes and lifted his latte to his mouth, choosing not to share what he thought of the sunny monstrosity sitting atop his girlfriend's head. He might not know much about women, but he knew enough.

"And if you must know, I'm incognito, okay? This hat is my disguise."

He scoffed. "For what? A Xanadu reunion tour?"

"I'm going to stuff you into a garbage can, Kovalev."

"You know, when I thought you'd talk dirty to me, that's not quite what I imagined."

"All this is critical to this caper stakeout."

"How?"

"It's hiding my pink hair. Hello! People would see that a mile off."

"You have an actual flower on your head," he said.

She pulled a face. "And?"

He bit his lip. "It's yellow and the size of your head."

"That's your opin—" She sat up straight and then leaned over to grab his hand. "Quick! Look like we are on a date," she hissed at him as she sank low in her seat.

"Shouldn't be hard, since I thought that was the actual reason we came here."

"Don't pout. It's caper time."

Grace's order fell on deaf ears as Anton hunched over his coffee with a barely muffled growl. She inclined her head.

"Did you just growl?" she asked. The noise hadn't been unpleasant. In fact, it had shot right through her to her toes.

"What of it, shortcake?"

"Put this on." Grace slid a hat—blessedly, not a knot

flower beanie—at him. Nevertheless, he took one look at it and scowled.

"I'd rather be sucked out of an airlock into deep space."

"Fine, but if the jackwagon from your lab recognizes us then I'm blaming you."

"Wait? What?" Anton sat up in his chair and, to Grace's horror, he turned and looked at said suspect.

"That's Jones from development." Anton flicked a finger at the man studying the menu. He was in his mid-30s and rather nondescript. Everything about the man made Grace think of bland oatmeal and unseasoned chicken breasts.

She wrinkled her nose. He wasn't a bad-looking man, just forgettable, which made him a prime suspect. Well, that and the fact that she had caught the man snooping in Lou's office that morning.

"Looking for a pen," he'd said, holding up one of the many Bic pens littering Lou's desk. He'd slipped from the room, muttering something about inventory reports, and on any other day she might have let the encounter slip her mind.

Now, as she honed in on him with all the accuracy and intensity of a homing missile, she thought there was something not quite right about a man who could vanish into a crowd, a man so plain he made vanilla ice cream seem daring. She had seen enough Cold War spy movies to know when a double agent was afoot.

She wasn't sure what to expect, and truth be told she would be amazed if the timid little man had it in him to orchestrate and carry out the theft of their data, but weirder things had occurred in her life. Her gaze strayed from Jones to Anton, who still glared at the trucker hat she had thrust at him.

She was now the girlfriend of a billionaire. Indeed, stranger things had been known to happen than Jones being a mole.

"Why the hell do you think Jones is the thief?" Anton asked, slipping the hat on. Only then did she deign to answer him.

"Because he's like oatmeal," she said.

Anton leaned close to her, elbows on the table, knee brushing against hers in a way that made her pulse speed up.

Okay, *maybe* her little stakeout had the potential to end in smooching. She found herself leaning toward Anton as he spoke, her mind dancing with memories of the growl he'd just let loose.

"Going to need you to elaborate on the breakfast food parallel."

"He can vanish like a damn ninja, and even though I've been staring at him all day I would probably forget what he looked like in a second."

"How did you know that was him, then?"

"I took a photo for reference, duh." She held up her phone, which displayed a photo of Jones taken at a haphazard angle below his chin. The outline of Grace's finger could be seen on the corner of the photo.

"Where did you get that?"

"Took it this morning in the labs when I handed out coffee. Pretended to trip and snapped it when he caught me."

Anton gave her a look of concern. "Grace..."

"Yes, I know. I was straight up creepin', but who cares? The bigger issue is that I caught him in Lou's office this morning, and that's why we're here."

"He was in Lou's office?" Suddenly Anton went sharp-eyed. Shooting a furtive look over his shoulder, he yanked the hat lower on his head. "What was he doing in there?"

"Said he was looking for a pen." She held up a hand. "And before you say 'that's totally normal,' he was spooked when I caught him and hightailed it out of there at top speed."

"A pen, you say?"

"Yes, a pen."

"Jones doesn't use pens."

"What?" she whisper-screamed.

"Avoids them at all cost. Drives the rest of us insane. Graphite and wood kinda man." Anton shook his head. "Makes a godawful mess, with him being left-handed."

"So the pen excuse is—"

"Suspect."

"Well, hot damn." Grace rubbed her hands together, the flower on her beanie bouncing as she hummed in excitement.

Her caper was already off to a success.

They watched as Jones ordered a pumpkin spice latte. Who knew oatmeal-man Jones liked to treat himself? He pulled out a pencil and sketchbook and began to draw. Grace bit her lip and slumped forward in her seat, knitted flower drooping in a mirror of her posture.

"What's wrong?" Anton chuckled at the forlorn expression on her face.

"He's not being diabolical." She rubbed her temples in

frustration. "You should have seen him this morning. He scuttled, Anton. Scuttled like a guilty little crab."

"Let me see your list." He extended a hand. "You weren't wrong about thinking it was odd that he was in Lou's office looking for one of those godawful plastic things she loves so much. You keep things well-stocked in the labs. He didn't need to go in there, and he is newer to my team."

"Meaning?"

"Meaning that I haven't gotten to speak to him outside of reports. Mindy selected him for the position, not me." He tapped the table again. "Now hand over the list. I know you have one for this whatsit plan you have."

"Caper," she supplied, already pulling out a folded piece of paper. Anton took it, his dark eyes moving down the names before he stiffened and his mouth pressed into a thin line. He looked up at Grace, who watched Jones sketch.

"Everyone on this list is a member of my team."

"Huh?" She looked away from Jones, who had begun staring into space as he drank his latte.

Were there sinister and thiefish thoughts running through his bland-looking head? There had to be something diabolical going on in there.

"I said, everyone on this list is a member of my team. You want to explain that?"

She slid to the side in her booth seat, already deciding to get up and take a closer look at Jones's sketch pad. Maybe there was a telling clue she could glimpse, or maybe the man had just been drawing deranged stick figures...the universe only knew, but she, Grace Muñoz, Lab Queen, was going to find out.

"Grace." The sharp tone of Anton's voice stopped her from standing. She froze in that awkward place between sitting and standing that made her look like a hunchbacked troll, and she gave him a confused look.

"What?" she asked, still not moving from her half-squat Nosferatu posture.

"Why is everyone on this list from my team?"

"Because I don't know them?"

"But I do," Anton huffed.

"You just said you didn't know Jones." She nodded to the man, who still stared at a spot on his table. "He scuttles. They were guilty scuttles. I saw them. And I'm going to see what he's drawing."

She began to stand straight when Anton surprised her by stepping past her.

"Where are you going?" she asked when he pulled the hat from his head.

"To think," he muttered, handing her the hat and shaking his head.

"But Jones..."

"Is still a part of the team, just like the other fifteen people you have on that list, and that isn't okay. Why didn't you at least tell me who you were looking at when you made that list?"

"I, ah, well... I thought you might be too partial to them."

"And you're not partial to yours?"

"Anton, come on." She reached a hand out toward him, but he had already stepped back.

"Have fun with whatever this is." He gestured toward Jones's table.

Jones, at that moment, snapped out of his stupor and realized that his boss and Grace were only a few feet away. He straightened up, hands going to his sketch pad, which Grace noticed he snapped shut right away.

Anton raised a hand in greeting before he turned. "Call me later, Grace," he called out as he left the coffee shop.

"He wasn't looking for me about the reports I haven't filed, right?" The man managed to look unflustered even in the wake of her flailing.

"Reports? W-what reports?" she said once she had managed to get her heart rate under control.

"I forgot to get my weekly report in, but I mean, it was just settling in and customs stuff..." Jones said, running a hand through his hair. "I didn't think it was that big a deal. Mindy told me it was okay."

"Yeah, I'm sure it was," Grace said.

"You have a flower on your head."

"Yeah? And?" She straightened up, giving him a challenging look.

"I think it's neat."

Grace frowned. "Oh...thank you."

"No problem. Well, I guess I'll go back to my table. Tell Mr. Kovalev I'll get the reports to him first thing. Have a nice day."

"I will. Thanks, you too." She watched Jones amble back to his table and reopen his sketch pad without a care in the world.

"Have a nice day? My hat is neat?" Grace whispered to herself with a groan.

What was she doing? Jones was perfectly nice. A little bland, like oatmeal, but oatmeal was nutritional and part of a healthy diet. Where had she gotten off thinking he was a thief just because he was a tad boring?

Pulling her hat off her head with a yank, she stomped out of the coffeehouse and onto the sidewalk. Turning from side to side, she looked for Anton.

Maybe he hadn't gone very far yet?

"You really did it this time," she muttered to herself.

Of course Anton was upset that she had focused on his team. She would have been the same, if the roles had been reversed.

No, she would have been 9 billion times worse. She would have been livid, furious, and irrational at best if someone had proposed that her team harbored a thief. They were her tribe—she loved and cared for each of them with the utmost attention and adoration, and would have been prepared to duel anyone who questioned their innocence.

She would have been an unholy terror of the first order had Anton done what she had just done. But he hadn't done that. No, instead he had remained level-headed and excused himself.

She twisted the hat in her hands in frustration at the wounded look in his eyes.

"Why didn't you at least tell me who you were looking at when you made that list?"

"Because I'm an actual idiot that doesn't know how to do feelings," she huffed. She pulled out her phone and sucked in a deep breath. She owed him an apology—oh, man, did she ever.

Can I come over later? she texted with all the nervousness of a middle schooler. Who knew that in a relationship with a former rake and renowned playboy, she would be the terrible communicator?

Classic.

A gentle ping in her phone made her freeze mid-stomp. She swallowed hard and set her foot down before taking out her phone to see the message from Anton.

Eight okay?

That was three hours from now. Not near enough time for her to figure out how to take her foot out of her mouth.

Perfect. See you then, Grace fired back. She had approximately 180 minutes, or 10,800 seconds, to figure out how to make things right between herself and Anton, and there wasn't a moment to lose.

CHAPTER ELEVEN

*"*S*CIENCE AND EVERYDAY life cannot and should not be separated."*

—Rosalind Franklin

THE HINGES on Anton's hotel room door had only begun their slide when Grace spoke. "I was out of line earlier."

He blinked, caught off-guard by the sight in front of him. It wasn't an uncommon thing for women to appear at his door, but one had never quite done it like Grace.

She held a large bouquet of flowers, white tulips to be exact, because roses were outplayed and an internet search had informed her that white tulips were the perfect flower for the occasion.

10,800 seconds had come and gone and the only solution Grace trusted herself to carry out was to apologize.

With flowers. Everyone loved flowers.

"You got me flowers?" He took the bouquet with a furrowed brow.

"Well, yes." Grace ran her hands through her hair, not quite sure what to do with them now that they were free. "I'm sorry and, ah, white tulips mean you're sorry and you want a fresh start. I googled it and everything."

Anton grinned, his eyes on the bouquet in his hand. "Come on in." He stepped back from the door.

Following him into his hotel suite, she let out a whistle. She had been expecting a simple room, maybe a little nicer than normal, but she hadn't been prepared for this. A long hallway with dark hardwood floors lined with actual, honest-to-goodness art, led to an open-concept space divided into a living room, dining room, and kitchen. Floor-to-ceiling windows, comfy couches perfect for napping in style, and trendy knick-knacks made the space feel lived-in, not impersonal.

A door in the far corner of the room made her wonder if it led to his bedroom, but before she could investigate her mouth dropped open at the sight of the bookcases lining the wall.

"You have a library? Real books?" She leaned close, surprised to see actual titles from the likes of Austen and Twain among the collection.

Anton stood at the kitchen counter, staring at the bouquet. "It's one of my requirements. I need something other than television, or I'll lose it. Have to unplug, and I'm too lazy to go to a bookstore."

"This place is amazing." It made her small apartment look like a postage stamp. A very well-kept and cheery postage stamp, but a postage stamp nonetheless.

"Thanks. Makes it easier being away from home. No

one has ever gotten me flowers before, so I'm not really sure what to do with them now."

"You generally put them in water."

"A giant bowl or pitcher or something?" He began rummaging around. "Help a guy out here. If you're going to flip the gender role script on me, then I need some guidance."

Grace grinned. "I'll help. We need a vase. I guess I didn't think about logistics when I got the flowers." She gave him an apologetic look, but he waved a hand.

"That just means we get creative," he said, moving into the living room. He snatched up what Grace thought was a ceramic sculpture painted in gold leaf and embedded with glass. "This will work."

"But that's art. You can't jus—" Grace began, but the words dried up when Anton rolled his eyes and began to fill the sculpture with water.

"Art is meant to be functional," he told her with a shrug.

"But won't the hotel get mad?"

"Nah." He shook his head, settling the flowers into the art piece-turned-vase. "I own this chain.'

"You what?!"

"The hotel. I own it. Why else do you think I'm staying here?"

"I don't know? Bachelor reasons?" She shrugged and then shook her head. "Wait a minute. How do you just own a hotel chain in Geneva?"

"My family has acquired properties for decades, and my mother always had a soft spot for this city," he said, as if it were the most normal thing in the world.

She let out a little laugh and shook her head. It was a reminder of how different their upbringings—their worlds—had been. There had been little joy or pleasure in her family.

She swallowed, mind skittering over the dark memories of her childhood. There had never been softness. No apologies. Her parents had never failed to remind her just how soft she was.

How unnecessary she was.

How sorry. Useless.

Anton gave her a questioning look, and she chewed on her bottom lip in favor of the frown threatening to burst forth. She had shown up to apologize, not brood. What was wrong with her?

"That's..." She tilted her head to the side and worked to pick the right words. "Impressive."

"Is it?" Anton asked as he focused on arranging the flowers in the vase.

"Well, yes."

"I didn't do it though." His dark eyes flicked up to meet hers. "My family did. I just got lucky."

She leaned against the counter. She was more than a little caught off guard by his response. Usually when someone disclosed something like he had, there was a tad more pride in their eyes, even if they tried to downplay it.

But that wasn't the case with Anton. He looked almost frustrated by it.

"Oh?" she asked, eyes rapt on his face as he shrugged and went back to fiddling with the flowers.

"I've been incredibly lucky in my life. The resources I've had at my fingertips, the things I've taken for granted, are more than most people have in a lifetime," he replied, turning the vase around on the counter in front of him. "What do you think?"

"I think you're right. You can do anything in the world. I mean, anything at all, and I'm not exaggerating. You have been given the world—no, the universe—in terms of money and power and influence. People have to listen to you, or at least the people you work with, because hello! You own the company. I mean, it's their job to listen to you."

He nodded at the vase. "I meant about the flowers."

"Oops." She ran her hands over her face and let out a low moan of frustration. "I'm sorry. I'm so sorry. *Again.*"

If only the floor would open up and swallow her whole.

But miracles like that weren't likely, so she was stuck standing on firm ground and blushing. He arched an eyebrow at her, but there was a wry smile on his lips.

"I think the flowers will look good over here." He nodded at the end table beside the sofa. "Don't you think?"

"I, well, yes."

She crossed her arms and watched as Anton ambled over to the end table with the vase of flowers. He seemed so nonchalant about her comments regarding his status in life. The people she worked with had strong and even visceral and explosive reactions to the merit of pens versus pencils. But here Anton was, unfazed when she laid out his advantages in life.

She shuffled forward, mouth opening and closing.

"Stop expecting me to bite your head off. You're right

about what you said. It's why I give so much of my good fortune away," Anton told her, his back to her still. "I may be privileged but I'm not oblivious. I try to use what I have for good."

That stopped her in her tracks. "What are you talking about?"

"A little of this and a little of that. Are you hungry? I'll have something sent up, or we can go out."

"Just like that? You're just forgiving me?" she ventured, fingers twisting in her sweater.

He nodded. "Just like that. And besides, if memory serves me right, you forgave me when I was an asshole."

She tilted her head to the side and considered him for a long beat. "Are you sure you want to date me?"

"You just listed out the number of ways in which I am beholden to no one, didn't you?" he asked. He crossed his arms as he waited for her answer, and she shifted from foot to foot as she tried to figure out where he was going, so she nodded.

"Yes, that's right."

"So where in all of that did you get the idea that I have ever done a damn thing I didn't want to do?"

"Well, it's just that you're you and I'm me." She waved a hand in a sweeping gesture at herself, from the top of her pink-tinted hair to her beaten up boots. There was no denying they were different.

"What does that mean?"

"I'm just not…refined," she said.

"I know. That's why I like you."

She jerked in surprise. "What's that supposed to mean?"

He rolled his eyes. "Oh, don't get defensive. I recognize that tone from twenty paces. I meant it as a compliment."

"Explain."

"I mean, I like you as you are. I like that you speak your mind. I like that you don't worry about getting your hands dirty and that you get me flowers when you apologize."

She bit her lip. "You like the flowers?"

He laughed. "Yeah. I think I understand the appeal of them, now that someone's given me a bouquet of my very own."

"They brighten up the place," she said.

"Just like you," he said, coming to stand beside her. "You make this place...nicer. I think you could make everywhere nicer."

She sucked in a deep breath when his fingertips brushed her jaw, just barely skimming as he ran a finger up to tuck her hair behind her ear.

"You're the only real thing I've had in my life for a while, Grace."

"No, Anton, th—"

"Shh," he murmured and leaned in close to her so that his lips pressed against her temple. "You are. Now listen to me. That's your job, remember?"

Grace laughed and leaned against him as she blinked away tears. "I don't work for you. I work for Lou. You're just visiting."

"I'll have to buy the facility immediately and have that changed." His hands moved to cup her cheeks, and he tilted her head back so that he gazed down at her. Their bodies pressed so close that hers moved in tandem with his as he breathed. She raised her hands up to his biceps, fingers wrapping around the muscles she found there.

"You can't buy CERN," she whispered, breath syncing up with his so seamlessly that she swore what they were doing could be considered mediation. She felt the earlier tension rolling off her body as they inched closer, bodies fitting together like puzzle pieces.

"I don't like being told what to do," he said, his eyes dropping to her mouth. He leaned close to her, and her lips parted in anticipation of the kiss she knew was coming.

Their opportunities for kisses had been few and far between, and this kiss was long overdue.

Odin, she wanted to climb him like a redwood, and only managed to hold herself in check because of the yoga voodoo magic their breathing had worked.

"So I've been told," she managed to get out before his lips brushed hers. Their kiss was tentative at first, sweet in its uncertainty. Anton's hands were gentle as they combed through her hair, and he slanted their mouths together after another gentle brush of their lips to kiss her deeper.

A low moan in her throat made him pull her tighter, kissing her deeper and whispering her name against her lips with all the care of a prayer. Men didn't handle her like she was fine china, they didn't kiss her with passion that made her toes curl or her breath catch in her throat.

Men didn't do any of this with her.

But Anton did.

CHAPTER TWELVE

"The very nature of science is discoveries, and the best of those discoveries are the ones you don't expect."

-Neil deGrasse Tyson

Anton popped his knuckles and sighed, looking out at the night skyline, tapping and twirling the heavy silver pen between his fingers. It was quiet in his apartment, Grace having gone to bed, and the clicking of the pen was comforting to him, a blessing as Anton couldn't stop his hands from moving.

It was a nervous habit. Something he did when he didn't want to think or speak. He'd learned to be silent when he'd enrolled at MIT. In those early days, it was easy to go ages without using his voice, and he found he welcomed the quiet, so long as he didn't look too hard at himself.

His first few months at MIT, Anton had kept his head

in his books, his nose clean, and nearly every free hour alone, dreaming or inventing new tech capable of keeping up with his ever-changing needs.

From the beginning, there never seemed to be anything that quite fit what he searched for.

Despite his reputation as a partier and attention-seeker, Anton had never been good with people, and trying to explain what he wanted to accomplish to the other students, who barely took him seriously, really wasn't his cup of tea. He knew the professors were confused at his presence in their classes.

At first, they moved over him as if expecting him to be playing on his phone rather than taking copious notes, but nearly immediately they noticed his unwavering attention and bit by bit he earned their acceptance. He even became a favorite of some faculty members, which pleased him more than he let on. His cohort took longer to come around, not that it bothered him.

Being left alone suited him just fine. Too many people looking to him for attention, or worse, giving him attention, had pushed him down a dangerous path littered with booze, women, and impulsive decisions.

The quiet was fine. The solitude was welcome. It meant more time for productivity. He did his best thinking when things were still. When he could just be and breathe.

But now the silence was anything but.

Now Anton found the silence oppressive. His fingers twirled the pen again, hand bouncing against his thigh as he shifted in his seat. His eyes landed on Grace, asleep in his bed, her pink hair spread out around her like a cotton candy halo on the pillows.

Anton sucked his bottom lip between his teeth and blew out a hard breath through his nose. After a takeout feast and some heavy cuddling, they'd passed out in his bed with a B-level horror movie on in the background. It'd been too easy to fall asleep with her in his arms, her heartbeat echoing his own, her body pressed against his side.

Anton couldn't remember the last time he'd simply lain in bed with another person, let alone a woman he was attracted to. He had enjoyed his time with women, but things always seemed less intimate, less vulnerable in those encounters. He'd been content to hold her until they'd both fallen asleep. Anton had awoken an hour or so later, disoriented, before the evening had all come back in a rush to him.

His chest ached, feeling full at the sight of her. Her mouth was slightly open, her face smushed into a pillow. Anton thought she was cute. Adorable, even.

It was terrible.

He spun the pen faster and frowned, looking away from her. Looking away from the only woman he'd ever managed to date seriously. He shook his head at himself and rubbed his temples with his free hand. What the hell did that say about him? A man in his early thirties, and he'd never been anyone's significant other.

"What the fuck?" he whispered, squeezing his eyes shut. "What the actual fuck?"

He padded out of the bedroom so as to not wake Grace with his existential crisis.

His feet carried him straight to his liquor cabinet. He shifted in front of it, eyes moving over the selection before he snatched a bottle of black label whiskey off the shelf and poured himself a glass. The liquid burned his throat when he threw it back, and he winced. It was a drink meant to be sipped, not shotgunned like he was a witless frat boy, but it couldn't be helped.

He turned, eyes landing on the bouquet of white tulips she'd brought him earlier that day, and he walked over to the flowers, catching a petal between his fingers. Their fragrance was beautiful, lovely even, just like Grace.

The thought made him frown, and he took a quick stutter-step away from the flowers. He well and truly liked his girlfriend.

"What am I going to do?" he whispered. He'd really gone and done it now. His inability to turn away from a challenge had led him down the path of destruction more than once, and now just look at him. He never learned his lesson, he never stopped to think—

"Anton?"

He spun around like a top to see her standing in the doorway of his bedroom. Her pink hair was a mess around her shoulders, her clothes rumpled, and not even the threat of morning breath could make him not think she was cute when she rubbed at her eyes with the back of her hand.

How did normal people deal with this?

Anton took in a deep breath and forced himself not to not pull out his hair in frustration. It wasn't Grace's fault. He couldn't even keep a houseplant alive, and somehow he was now tied to another human being. An actual person's emotional well-being had been entrusted to him, and as much as he hated it, he knew his heart was in Grace's hands, too.

Hers to crush into a million little pieces.

Anton swallowed hard and gave her a little smile. "Yeah?"

"Where did you go?"

"Business call," Anton said, willing himself to stop staring at her like a lovesick fool. He was an experienced man-about-town, who had sought refuge from his jaded existence in science, so why was he floundering like a teenager being confronted by their first love?

"Really?" she asked, taking a step into the room.

He gave her a nod. "Truly."

She crossed her arms and kept walking toward him. "Are you coming back to bed or should I go?"

Her eyes darted to the side, toward the door, and Anton's heart squeezed. He hated that he'd been the one to put that look of uncertainty on her face.

He had to fix it.

"Don't be silly." He waved his hand at her, giving her his best reassuring smile. "Go back to bed. I'll be there soon."

"Are you sure?" She shifted from foot to foot, but she stopped where she was, just a few feet away from him. It took everything in him to not cross the space and pull her close, to run his hands over her and bury his face in her hair like he wanted to. Instead he gave her a smile that he knew didn't quite reach his eyes.

"Of course. I'll be along soon. I just...need to finish a few things."

"Okay…"

Her fingers twisted in her shirt, and she looked dubious in response to his answer, but after another long beat she turned and made her way back to the bedroom. She paused at the door, one hand on the knob, looking over her shoulder at him.

He could tell she wanted to say something, but he watched as she swallowed it and disappeared into the bedroom. He sagged against the counter behind him and let out the breath he had been holding. With a shaky hand he put down the whiskey glass and shook his head.

He resisted the urge to pour himself another drink and rubbed a hand over his face. This was exactly what he got for rising to her bait.

Geneva was supposed to be a place for him to recharge and get over RED's theft, but what had he done? Fallen for the first attractive, smart mouthed, dark-eyed woman who had a penchant for getting under his skin like it was in her job description.

Instead of heading back to the bedroom, he sank onto the leather couch and put his head in his hands. There needed to be a support group for how he felt. For people who had no experience with intimacy realizing they were heading toward—love.

He blanched at the thought, eyes going to the door again where Grace had gone. Suddenly his bedroom didn't seem so safe and cozy, not when there was a woman behind it capable of sending his world into a tailspin.

He settled himself further into the couch. If he wanted to do this right, then there was no rushing it. He would collect his thoughts, come up with a solid plan, and execute it to the T.

The next time he opened his eyes it was to an annoyed *(and cute, god help him)* Grace, who glared down at him.

"Business call, huh?"

"Uh..." Anton's mind was blank except for one thought: She was angry at him, which was fair—and obvious, since he had fallen asleep on the couch.

"Uhh?" Grace parroted, one hip coming out in a pose he recognized from Mindy. It was the universal sign that she was pissed, and his brain shorted out. An angry girlfriend? He didn't even know how to deal with a regular girlfriend.

So, he panicked.

"Go away with me," he blurted out, the words tumbling over one another so fast they gave him whiplash.

She blinked in surprise. "What? Away? Like, for the weekend?"

His head bobbed and he pushed himself up from the couch. "Yes. Away. Out of here for the weekend. Just the two of us. What do you think?"

Almost instantly she relaxed. "That could be fun," she replied, a shy smile on her face.

His breath left him in a whoosh. He was forgiven for staying away last night, but he had also thrown away his master plan of keeping it cool in favor of making her happy.

Where was he even going to take her? His mind

skipped ahead, considering the details, but a second later his thoughts dissolved under the brightness of her smile.

"I think it could be really fun. I'm excited." She darted forward, pressing a kiss against his cheek, and he almost groaned at himself

He knew he was done for.

CHAPTER THIRTEEN

"If you do high-level science, everything is a challenge."
—Maria Leptin

"What do you mean you're 'going away for the weekend'? Where? With whom?" Lou's barrage of questions cracked through her apartment like a shot from the speaker of Grace's cell phone.

Grace huffed out a sigh as she fixed herself a to-go mug of coffee. She bit her lip. Would Anton want coffee? Would it be rude to not have a cup for him when he picked her up in half an hour?

Jumping Jehoshaphat, what were the rules and regulations? When was she supposed to offer beverages? Did a trip out of the city count?

She shook her head and grabbed another to-go mug from her cupboard. Better safe than sorry. There was no reason for her not to bring him a cup, but what about snacks? Did that mean she needed to feed him?

She scrambled for her fridge in search of a snack that wouldn't make her appear like an unsupervised pre-teen with a debit card. She had to have something nutritious, not covered in chocolate or cut into a dino shape.

So sue her, she liked a good Tyrannosaurus after a hard day, but who didn't?

On second thought, chocolate wouldn't be so bad—she could work with chocolate. Chocolate was sexy, right?

"GRACIE?!" Lou yelled from the phone, making Grace wince. She had forgotten about her best friend on speaker.

Major oops.

Though it was hard to stay focused when she was thinking about what was under Anton's sweaters and perfectly tailored pants. She'd managed to get her hands on him last night, and all she could say was whoa mama. The man was toned and cut, which she had suspected from the fashionable stretch of his clothing. She would put money on the fact that he had a full gym in his lab he hit every day of the week.

There was no way Anton spent the hours in his lab, at least not like Lou had said...

Grace frowned.

Lou...LOU!

She had forgotten about Lou again!

"GRACIE, I SWEAR TO GOD," Lou screeched at full pterodactyl strength.

"Sorry." Grace jerked her head up and tried to reach for the phone, but only succeeded in almost knocking herself unconscious by slamming face-first into the fridge door. "Fuck."

"What the hell is going on over there?" Lou asked, voice fading in and out as Grace swayed.

"Just trying to—give me a sec, okay?"

Grace braced her hands on the counter and shook her head. Being a girlfriend was hard. She would be lucky if she survived the weekend. She rubbed her head and sighed, grabbing a bag of trail mix which was only mostly chocolate and grabbed her phone.

"I'm going away with Anton."

"What was all that banging and cursing?"

"Me trying to girlfriend while talking to you on the phone."

"It sounded like you almost died."

"Very nearly," Grace muttered, throwing the trail mix in her bag with a grimace. "I wasn't sure if I should feed him. I mean, I'm bringing coffee and that's normal, right?"

There was a beat of silence before Lou giggled.

"Oh, Gracie."

"Don't *oh Gracie* me. I'm serious about this. No one ever tells you what to do when you get a boyfriend or what to do when you go away together, alright? This is all new. I'd rather be staring at one of your ridiculous theorems than doing this. At least there are rules there."

Lou blew out a heavy sigh. "Relationships aren't about rules, Gracie. You don't have to check off things nice and neat, okay? Relax and enjoy Anton. It's all about getting to know one another, not keeping order. Just be you. You don't have to be perfect. He isn't going to hold it against you that you don't know what you're doing. This isn't like home."

Grace went still, her fingers tightening around the

coffee mug she had been about to pour coffee into, her eyes dropping to the countertop at Lou's last words.

This isn't like home.

She didn't have to be perfect, though that need to pretzel-twist herself into whatever best suited the comfort of those around her still weighed on her shoulders. She'd always been a chameleon: at home in Arizona, in the classrooms of her university where no one quite looked like her, and now in the meetings with other directors of research or at the dressy galas she and Lou had to attend. It would have been a lot for her, even without the added hurt from her family life, which had been less like a home and more like a tomb.

Grace cleared her throat and went back to the task of pouring Anton coffee. She'd much rather prepare for the trip than remember exactly what *before* meant.

"When did you become the relationship whisperer, huh? I'm supposed to be the one who reminds you that you're not a robot bent on science domination."

Lou scoffed. "Look, I can people. Just because I don't like doing it with very many people doesn't mean that I can't do it. And for you? I would people so hard."

Grace blinked back against the tears that welled up in her eyes. "Thank you for peopling for me," she choked out. "You're the best friend a woman could ask for."

"Don't I know it," Lou said and then added, "but so are you, Gracie."

"Love you," Grace sniffled, wiping her tears away before they could do much damage to the natural but hopefully sexy eye makeup she had painstakingly applied for the first leg of her weekend away with Anton. If her makeup was flawless then he wouldn't notice what a nervous wreck of a woman she was. She couldn't ruin hours of experimenting with YouTube makeup tutorials with tears. Not when Anton was due to pick her up any minute.

"Stop crying, damn you. You're going away on a romantic weekend, not a death sentence to the gallows. He's going to think you're nuts if you walk out crying," Lou chastised her.

Grace rolled her eyes and dabbed at them. "Thanks for the tip, mom."

"Anytime, darling. Now go get yourself together and enjoy this weekend."

"Are you sure you're okay without me?" Grace asked.

Things had been tense since the data had been stolen, and she was still leery of running away for a weekend without Lou.

"I don't have to go, you know? We can stake out the labs and catch the asshole who stole the data."

"Don't worry about a thing back here. I'm going to be fine."

"But y—"

"No. I mean it, Gracie. I want you to go and enjoy this weekend. I'm a big girl. I can handle this. The data is still going to be stolen when you get back, and I promise that you can go absolutely wild trying to find the thief when your little romantic getaway is over."

"Do you promise?"

"Cross my heart. I'll even help, but I draw the line at getting arrested."

"That was one time."

"Once is enough. We're lucky it was local authorities who took us in, you know." Grace pulled a face at the reminder and stuck her tongue out when Lou began to drone on about the importance of following local authorities, even if and especially when trespassing was involved.

"You know, I think I like doling out the chastisements," Grace told her, scooping up her duffle bag and trying to balance the two coffees in her hands when she saw the text notification announcing Anton's arrival.

"Gotta take it if you're gonna dish it out," Lou said.

"Uh huh," Grace said, shoving the cell phone between her shoulder and chin while she reached for the front door. "I gotta run, boss lady best friend. Anton is outside and—"

Grace jerked open the door and stopped speaking when she came face-to-face with Anton, who stood with one fist raised to knock on her front door.

"What are you doing here?" Grace blurted out, surprised at his sudden appearance.

"Oh, good morning to you too, dear," Anton said with a shake of his still-raised fist. "Is one of those for me?" He gestured at the mugs in her hands.

"Yupparoo." Grace handed the mug to him.

"What's going on over there?" Lou asked, startling Grace.

"Anton's at the door."

"Awww, how cuuuuute." Lou's sing-song voice in ear would have made Grace cringe, or even fire off a smart-mouthed retort, but now it just made her blush.

"Yes, he is," she said instead, making Lou let out a

squeak of shock at her frank response, "and I have to go. Like now."

"Fine, go and enjoy. Call me when you're back."

"Of course. Love you too, mom." Grace smiled at Anton and ended the call as fast as she could. He smirked at her, sipping from his mug as she struggled to lock the door.

"Nervous?" he purred, leaning over her shoulder so that his lips grazed her ear.

She jolted up with a squeak. "What? No. Of course not," she answered at a volume hardly acceptable for indoors. "Why would I be nervous?"

Anton shrugged. "You tell me. You're the one blushing and breathless."

"Preposterous."

He said nothing and followed her as she stomped down the hallway. He flashed her a grin when she glanced back at him. "I'm not nervous," she insisted, shoving open the front door to her apartment building.

"Sure thing." He gave her a little salute before he stepped forward and nodded at the car. "I believe you."

"Shut up and drink your coffee," she ordered as she made a show of getting in the car with as unaffected an air as possible. He rounded the car with a laugh and she fished out the trail mix and held it out to him. "And eat this."

"Why?" he asked, taking the trail mix and eyeballing it before he turned on the car.

"Because it's what you're supposed to do."

"It is?"

"Yes, because I brought the snacks."

"And the coffee. Thank you."

"You're welcome. Now eat."

He shook his head and shoved a handful of trail mix in his mouth. "This is all chocolate," he said.

"It was either that or dinosaur chicken nuggets."

"You didn't have to bring snacks, but thank you."

"What do you mean?"

"I mean, you don't have to take care of me."

Anton's reply made her freeze. "What do you mean?"

He glanced toward her. "You're always taking care of everyone. You don't have to do that with me."

"I'm not always taking care of everyone," she replied, but then she scrunched up her face. "I mean, I don't think... Am I always taking care of everyone?"

"Yes." He ate another handful of trail mix as he navigated through the city. "I'm not saying it's bad that you do. I know you care about them, but it's got to be exhausting, right?"

She shook her head. "No, I love to do it. I don't really see it as taking care of people. It's just what I do. I'm the lab manager. I manage the lab, and that includes the scientists."

"I've had more than a few lab managers, and trust me. That's not what they do. You make the labs a home."

"Well, isn't it?" She leaned back in her seat and cradled her coffee mug.

"Isn't it what? A home?" He pulled a face. "I've never—until seeing you and yours—thought of a lab as anything but a place of business. It's where I go to work, not live. I've never done anything but be manic and drink coffee in my lab."

She turned over his words and sipped her coffee. What he was describing sounded foreign to her, but then again she had never had any lab experience until she'd become Lou's intern while living in Arizona and Grace didn't suppose the mechanic's garage had ever really constituted a lab other than in her and Lou's minds. Lou had always been content to let Grace run things as she saw fit. And that had meant making the lab into a home, a safe place to land, somewhere that everyone felt valued, seen, and heard. Grace had never seen the responsibility of making her people understand that they were, in fact, her people, a chore. It was something she enjoyed immensely. With all the moving around for work Lou's career now demanded it was a lovely feeling to not miss home because the labs and the minions within it were her home.

Though Grace supposed she'd never truly had much a home life. Her family had been distant, cold even, preferring to simply exist within the same walls than making a functioning family unit. She supposed that happened when said family lost a child.

Grace had been all of nine years old when her older sister, Lilia, had drowned. It hadn't been anyone's fault, it had just been one of those freak accidents you heard about on the news, felt bad for a moment about, and then moved on because it was a random family whose name you had already forgotten. Except in Grace's case it hadn't been a random family, it had been hers, and there hadn't been any moving on when her family had been forever changed one summer day at the community pool.

Lilia had been thirteen years old and Grace nine years old. Those four years had seemed like a lifetime of experience to Grace and she'd thought the older girl had hung the moon. Grace had been her shadow until Lilia hadn't been there to follow anymore.

From that day, it was like someone had sucked the light and love out of the Muñoz home. Grace had gone from the spoiled baby of the family to just been another checkbox to tick for them, not a real person with her own desires and personality. Her parents had fed, clothed, and gotten her to school but other than that they had little interest in her life and try as she might Grace had never been able to fit whatever it was her parents needed from her.

Her mother had laughed often and loudly before Lilia's death, so had her father, so had all of them. Or least that's what Grace's childhood memory told her. Sometimes she wondered if she had made up a world where everything had just been better when Lilia had been alive. Maybe her parents had always been dismissive, short-tempered and aloof and she was recalling those earlier days through rose colored glasses. Her doubt at a made up world only lasted for so long though and photos in the family albums that Grace only looked at when she was sure her parents were gone told her otherwise.

Things had been better when Lilia lived.

Those photos were proof. Proof that they had been better. All of them.

Without Lilia there had always seemed to be something missing from her parents' code in the way of warmth and nurturing. To make up for it Grace, it seemed, had inherited their measure of love and softness. Those special things Lilia had inspired-- laughter, hugs, and community were all things Grace craved and vowed to find again for herself. And while most women would have set out to find a partner, someone to love and marry, have a family, Grace had found what she'd wanted most with her place beside Lou and the science brigade. It was uncanny how effortlessly she'd fallen into it but now that she had she couldn't imagine her life without them. Her world, she'd even dare to say, was her role in looking after them.

"It's not taking care of. It's just...they need some help."

"You baby them."

She frowned at him. Wouldn't a sane person baby something if it was their whole world? Even still, she said, "I do not."

He turned onto the road that led out of the city and shook his head at her. "All I'm saying is you don't have to worry about me. I can fend for myself."

"I like doing it," she replied, voice soft. She lowered her eyes to her hands. "It's not work, or a bother, for me."

"You should be allowed to relax."

"I relax plenty."

"Is that why I found you sick under your desk a few days ago?" He glanced over at her.

"I have a lot of work to get done, you know?" she replied, eyes on the scenery outside.

"You need to remember to separate. It's going to burn you out at the rate you're going," he told her.

She hummed and looked away from the window. "There's not much time for rest. Not with the data thief on the loose. I have to be in the labs with Lou. She needs me."

Anton said nothing for a second. And when he spoke again, Grace felt like he had cut to the core of her. "It's okay to exist without them."

"What are you talking about?" She crossed her arms over her chest and did her best to keep her breathing even. Even as she asked the question she knew what he meant, because it was a guilt that she wrestled with constantly.

"They need you in their lives just as much as you need them in yours," he spoke up, breaking her from her thoughts. "There's no need to run yourself ragged trying to please everyone. They're adults."

She shook her head. "It's not that simple, okay?"

"Then tell me about it."

She flashed back to the last time she'd seen her parents, standing together on the front porch of their home in New Mexico, shoulder to shoulder, looking like twins rather than lovers. Their tired faces had been drawn tight, their mouths pressed into thin lines that she had willed to turn up, to mirror the smile on her own. It hadn't happened, and they stared at her blank-faced—but not without that air of exhaustion that always seemed to hang over her family.

As a child she had learned to be quieter, to speak softer and laugh at an acceptable volume. It seemed when she was more restrained her parents could be around her for longer, though they never seemed to really *see* her, not even then when she left for college.

Or even later when she came to tell them she was leaving for Geneva.

They had accepted the news with a nod and then

asked if she was hungry before excusing themselves and sitting down in front of the television. It had hurt, sitting in the kitchen and listening to the sound of the latest shitty sitcom blaring from the next room. That night, Grace had slipped from the house and decided to stop seeking approval from parents who barely seemed to recognize that they had a daughter. It was insane to keep looking to them for validation. She was going to have to make her own home, share her love and warmth with people smart enough to stay, and that was how the ragtag group of science misfits had come together under the behest of her wrangling powers. It had been rough at first, managing so many science-fascinated smartypantses, but she had found her stride, and now she couldn't think of life without them.

She sighed and turned to face Anton. She was treated to a view of his profile, and she let her eyes linger on him for an indulgent second. He was her boyfriend. He'd made sure she was taken care of when she was sick. Gone along with her science stakeout. Rescued a party for her. And now he was taking her away for the weekend.

She could almost pinch herself. How was this her life now? She couldn't even keep her own parents interested long enough to tell them about her new life.

"It's complicated," she said after perhaps staring just a little too long at him—so long, in fact, that he had cleared his throat and shot her a quick sidelong look that was universal code for: are you still there?

"Things are usually only complicated because we make them that way."

"Easy for you to say."

"Meaning?" he asked, and Grace didn't miss the strained tone that entered his voice. Just perfect. She always put her foot in her mouth when she thought about her family. They had the ability to make her feel like the insecure gawky teenager she'd once been—too bad she resorted to the same defensive coping mechanisms when she took a tumble down memory lane.

"Just—look, I'm sorry," she said. "I just mean that people have probably always wanted you around."

He drummed his fingers on the steering wheel. "And why wouldn't anyone want you around?"

"It's complicated. That's all. Can we just forget it?"

He made a noncommittal sound and they continued to drive on in silence. She forced herself not to fill the silence and looked back out the window.

She had a habit of chattering when she didn't need to. She'd gotten better at handling the silence, but now she practically choked on the words she wanted to spew. She fidgeted, hands going to tuck themselves beneath her when he said nothing and continued to drive. A few more seconds crawled by before she dared to glance in his direction.

His hands were steady on the steering wheel. His head was tilted, as if in contemplation, and she felt very near to passing out when he finally spoke.

"It's just that..." he began, voice trailing off as he sped up past a truck.

"Just that what?" she asked, unable to keep her mouth shut for another damn second.

"I just wish you would be gentler with yourself, Gracie."

She sucked in a breath. Tears welled up in her eyes and she blinked. “Okay,” she said, because she didn’t have any other words.

It was all too much. So she did what she did best and pasted on a chipper smile while dabbing at the corner of her eyes with her knuckles. “I think we need some music, don’t you?” she asked, hands already fiddling with her phone.

Anton didn’t protest or pry at her sudden change of direction. “Just no opera,” he said as their car continued to climb up the winding mountain road.

All of the prior tension in the car melted away. The biggest question Grace had to answer was how long and how loud she would blast Pavarotti.

CHAPTER FOURTEEN

"Physics isn't the most important thing. Love is."
—Richard P. Feynman

It was hard to say when Anton picked her up—it could have been halfway up the walkway to their chalet, or somewhere after he had kicked the door shut with all the energy of a Viking returning from a successful pillaging—but what Grace did know was that somehow she ended up in his arms, both legs wrapped around his waist, minus her jacket and with a shoe missing from one foot in some kind of R-rated retelling of Cinderella.

Okay, it wasn't just R-rated, it was bordering on the triple X-rated version of whatever wasn't decent to be seen while in the company of one's parents. The thought put a wide smile on her face and she pulled back to see that Anton had fared no better than she.

His normally styled hair was a mess, shirt rucked up and wrinkled—and his eyes, those gorgeous whiskey-brown eyes, had a frantic energy to them that filled her with a fire to see him come even more undone. There was just something about leaving a man out of breath and with swollen freshly kissed lips.

Forget Cinderella.

She was a Viking princess hellbent on having her man.

She surged forward, hands cupping his face as she went about kissing him as thoroughly as she could while still managing to yank his shirt up and over his head.

"Holy shit. You're a hellcat," he said in between kisses. She grinned and kicked off her remaining shoe so hard that it bounced off the wall with all the velocity of an errant cannonball. She giggled when the shoe landed next to them, but didn't stop in her quest to get him divested of his clothing.

The man was all fine lines of muscle and supple soft skin that her hands ached to trace and cover with kisses. Releasing his mouth with a sigh, she kissed her way across his jaw and down his neck, her lips burning a trail of small featherlight touches that left him panting.

"You're going to give me a heart attack," he whispered.

"Get a pacemaker."

"I'll have it added to my agenda." His hands began undoing the buttons of her jeans as he spoke, head tipped back as she continued to place kitten kisses on his skin. "First thing Monday morning, I'll look Mindy right in the eyes and tell her my cardiac health is at risk."

"Maybe don't talk about your assistant while I'm trying to get into your pants?"

He paused, tilted his head to the side as if her request

was new information, and then nodded. "Good point. Assistant talk bad."

She kissed him, her tongue tracing his bottom lip. "Very bad."

His hands continued to work on her jeans, and he pulled back eyeing her unbuttoned pants with a look of annoyance. The denim bunched around the tops of her thighs and his eyes zeroed in on the red lace that covered precious little of her lush thighs. He normally loved red on a woman, adored it and preferred it, in fact, but right now it incited him like a bull on a Barcelona street. He exhaled through his nostrils, the warm air tickling her skin as he crushed her close to him.

"You know what else is bad? Pants."

So focused on kissing his now bare shoulders was she that she missed the subtle change in his posture. If she had, she would have noticed he had assumed the stance of a man prepared to launch a projectile at top speeds. As such, her sudden airborne situation left her gasping and emitting the least sexy sound—a squeak, perhaps even a meep akin to something a Muppet might emit rather than a woman set on seduction.

She scrambled to sit up, her unbuttoned jeans open, shirt akimbo and hair wild as she gaped at Anton, who had begun yanking off his shoes. He stood in front of her, bare-chested and barefoot, one hand moving down to whip off his fine leather belt with a practiced hand that snapped the accessory against his thigh.

Grace sucked her bottom lip between her teeth at the crack of Anton's belt.

Boy oh boy.

What in the universe had she done to deserve such a treat? She was ready for the ravishing she appeared to be about to get.

"You tossed me in a manly fashion," she rasped, her vocal cords having forgotten their primary function.

He dipped his head in acknowledgment, his free hand trailing down his chiseled abs to graze the top of his pants.

"I did."

He looked up at her with a smoldering expression—like she was a nine-course dinner and he hadn't eaten in weeks. Like a wolf. She shuddered at the look of open desire in his eyes.

"And that's not all I'm going to do to you in a manly fashion."

The belt hanging from his fingers made her pulse jump at the base of her neck as a warm flush swept over her. If she was a Viking princess, then he was the king who was going to bring her to her knees.

"Come here."

He gestured with the belt before he let it fall from his fingers with a thud. She pushed herself up on her hands and knees and, keeping her eyes locked with his, crawled down the bed until she was in front of him. Leaning forward, she pressed a gentle kiss above his hip bone.

At the touch of her mouth, his body went rigid like a taut bowstring.

"You're so sexy," he whispered, his voice disrupting the quiet of the room. His hands tangled in her hair and she moaned, turning into his touch.

"I try," she murmured before dropping another kiss

against his side, higher this time, as her fingers began to explore the well muscled body of the man she was dead set on being thoroughly ruined by.

"Let me see you, Grace."

She went still then. He had said her name before, but *not like this.* This felt serious and complicated, intimate in a way that she didn't suppose she had any business experiencing.

But here they were.

And he'd said it: her name, uttered like a prayer. Something like that couldn't be happening between them; not yet, anyhow. It was too fast for something like that.

She could deny it all she wanted, but it didn't change the fact that they both knew. What he'd admitted to with that gentle, honey-sweet and silk-soft whisper of her name.

He couldn't take it back. She wouldn't let him.

Not a chance.

But that didn't mean she was 100% ready or qualified enough to deal with it. Not with her body raging at her to rip off his pants with her teeth and proceed to bang him like a screen door in a hurricane. What she wanted wasn't romantic—it wasn't even close to that ghost of a feeling she had picked up on when he'd said her name. Her body was screaming at her with only intentions of the dirtiest and most delicious kind.

No love. Just lust.

Her eyes widened at the thought: love. What the hell was she thinking? She gave a shake of her head and ripped off her sweater. She needed to stop thinking.

She reached out with hurried hands and undid the

button on his jeans. She had only just managed to unzip them when his hands came to rest on her shoulders, his touch gentle, and he lingered there, stroking her skin before he lifted his hands to her hair. Threading his fingers through her tresses, he spoke again in that soft timbre that had her bowing her head and shaking under his touch.

"Grace," he whispered.

"Mm?" She tucked her chin to her chest and kept her eyes on her hands, which fumbled at his pants.

By the gods, why were tear away pants only considered fashionable for exotic dancers? She would give anything for a length of convenient velcro and snap buttons.

"*Grace.* Darling."

Again with the soft voice that had her insides feeling molten. She bit her lip hard to keep from giving into it. One of his hands moved to cup her cheek, while the other fell to administering gentle strokes through her hair.

When she didn't immediately respond, he pushed her back an inch, taking her hands in his and stilling their feeble efforts to get his pants off. He sighed and pressed her fingers to his lips in a chaste kiss, so at odds with the needy and purely physical want Grace had been doing her best to lose herself in.

When she had imagined going to bed with the infamous Anton Kovalev, this hadn't been what she'd imagined. She smiled at the thought before letting loose a shaky breath and raising her eyes to his face. His eyebrows were knitted together in concern, eyes trained on hers, searching her out as she sat beside him.

"Are you okay with this? If you're not, if things have changed, it's okay."

"What? Why would you—I mean, what do you mean?"

"Your energy changed."

"Changed? I'm fine," she assured him with a watery smile. "Really. I think I'm just tired, you know, from the driving and capering this week."

Anton sucked his lips against his teeth and gave her a sidelong look. "Uh huh."

She crossed her arms over her chest, aware of how great it made her breasts look. Her cleavage was at full power, on display in the pretty red satin bra she had chosen for the occasion. She saw the way Anton's eyes dropped to her chest before darting back up to her face. Tossing her hair over her shoulder, she shimmied closer to him and shot him her best smile.

"Why don't you let me show you how fine I am, Mr. Kovalev?"

"In a sec."

Her mouth dropped open. What in the blue blazes did he mean? Just as she was about to make her displeasure known, he pressed a kiss to her forehead that stole the breath from her lungs.

"Don't give me that look. Be right back." He gave her a sweet smile before he bounded away from her with a wink and a hop. She blew her hair out of her face with an exasperated breath and flopped back onto the bed with a groan.

Her boyfriend had high-tailed it out of the room. How in the world did that happen?

She clenched her eyes shut and yanked a pillow over

her head. She really needed to reevaluate her approach to girlfriending, seeing as she had somehow missed the mark.

There had to be a manual out there. Maybe somewhere on the dark web?

The sound of footsteps approaching the bedroom pushed all thoughts of cryptocurrency and shady interwebz dealings from her head.

She tensed as his footsteps moved closer and closer until she knew he stood beside the bed. The pillow over her face offered a small measure of respite, though for how long she didn't know.

Maybe if she didn't move she could wait him out until dinner time.

"What are you doing?"

"Mrmph," she replied.

He put a hand up to his ear. "I'm sorry, what was that?"

Her hands clenched, but she made no move to push the pillow aside. "Mmmed mrrmph."

"I'm not fluent in pillow speak. You have to come out from under there at some point."

She sighed, her own breath hot on her face—which wasn't pleasant and became a deciding factor in her decision to push the pillow aside.

Otherwise, she might have made a real go at living out her days as the pillow-headed woman. If there were men with pumpkins for craniums then there was room in the world for a woman sporting bedding as a noggin.

Maybe if she breathed to the side for the rest of their weekend?

"Grace."

That one word made her let out one more hot sigh before she moved the pillow to the side. Odin, when had he learned to say her name like that? Did he practice when he should be sleeping? During his coffee breaks when no one was the wiser?

It was downright indecent.

"Yes?" she asked, doing her best to keep her voice even.

"Why did you hide?"

She noticed he carried what looked like a soft, fluffy cloud straight out of a video game or cartoon. She raised her eyebrow at the blanket, but when he cleared his throat realized he had asked her a question.

"What?"

"Why did you hide from me?" He inclined his head, a smile turning his lips up. "Not that it was the most creative disguise."

"I was desperate. It's all I had on hand."

"But why?"

"I felt silly."

"Silly? What?" He frowned, and reached a hand out to take hers, threading their fingers together. "Why did you feel silly?"

"It's nothing." She shook her head at him and then nodded at the fluffy cartoon cloud blanket. "What's that for?"

He didn't answer, and for a moment she worried he would press her to answer him, to admit that she had felt silly for feeling...rejected? She didn't know what she was trying to say, because rejection was so not what the man had inspired in her when he had whispered her name.

Before she could say anything he dropped the blanket

around her shoulders, and she had to fight not to melt into it like the Wicked Witch caught in a downpour. It was heavenly. She wasn't sure she'd ever had such luxurious fabric against her skin.

"Let's get some rest." He moved to push her back against the bed. She said nothing but watched with attention as he slipped her jeans from her hips, this time without any wandering fingers to make her blood heat up. His touch was gentle, caring...familiar in a way that made her heart ache for something she couldn't quite put into words.

She blinked back the tears that welled in her eyes as he moved around the room, dimming the lights and magicking another fluffy cloud blanket out of nowhere. She took the sleep shirt he offered her with a nod and, when he left the room, she got ready for bed.

She had just settled in when he returned with a mug of tea and a tablet under one arm. He handed her the mug, and when she eyed the tablet with curiosity he tossed it onto the bed next to her.

"Queue up one of those godawful trash programs I know you watch."

If she had been the Grinch her heart would have swelled to three times its size, but seeing as she was only human her heart nearly burst out of her chest.

He was taking care of her.

The man the media made out to have no heart was willing to watch reality television with her.

"I'll have you know I watch film noir and reruns of *Masterpiece Theatre,* so I have no idea what trash you're referring to, sir." She sipped from her cup while he pulled on a pair of sleep pants. He rolled his eyes at her and stretched his arms overhead, almost causing her to shatter her porcelain mug because he was a work of art. There wasn't an inch of him that didn't look like Michelangelo had forced him into being during a particularly inspired fit of creativity.

"Eyes up here," he said, though there was no mistaking the pleasure she saw as he strutted toward her.

"Someone's certainly full of himself," she muttered, but she didn't bother to look away from the muscles exposed to her eyes. She'd been caught—may as well window shop, right?

He smirked and slipped into bed beside her. She loaded up an awful French film she intended to watch to prove a point, but made it through no more than twenty minutes until she gave up and switched to her favorite housewives show.

So sue her—she had to keep abreast of current events, okay?

When she looked to see if Anton was judging her she only saw that he watched the screen with a rapt look on his face.

How did the man get more amazing every second? It was criminal.

Only after she had finished her tea and began to nod off did he nudge her onto her side and turn out the light. Her arms automatically closed around a pillow to fill the empty space beside her, but she froze when Anton pressed himself up against her back.

"Is this okay?" he whispered, breath warm against her ear. "Can I hold you?"

"Please," she murmured back without hesitation. A little sigh escaped her when he brushed her hair off her neck and pressed a kiss against the exposed flesh. And then he put his arm around her and pulled her tight to the curve of his body, and they slept in that special way lovers did when more than a little bit of pixie dust and magic had landed on them.

CHAPTER FIFTEEN

"Physics is like sex: sure, it may give some practical results, but that's not why we do it."

—Richard P. Feynman

"Why do you say that?"

Grace turned, looking up from the coffee she had been too impatient to wait for while it finished its brew time—which meant that she had unsuccessfully tried to swap her cup out for the carafe, only to be rewarded with a solid morning scalding.

"Say what?" she asked, wincing and shoving her hand under the tap while eyeballing her filling coffee cup. It wouldn't do to spill her cup onto the counter, not with the injury she'd just sustained, and she made a wild grab to shove the carafe back into place when her cup nearly overran with black gold. "Odin's beard," she muttered, sliding the cup closer to her with her uninjured hand.

"That," Anton said, coming into the kitchen. He leaned

against the counter and took out a mug to wait for the carafe to finish brewing, like a well-adjusted adult.

"Do what?" she asked again, shutting off the tap and drying her hands on her sweater. There wasn't time for towels when there was fresh-brewed coffee at hand. If she didn't have a cup soon, she was liable to give the science minions a run for their publication money.

"Odin's beard?" he asked. "I came in here to you yelling and I quote, 'by Thor's hammer.'"

She waved a hand. "Well, yeah, that burn was no joke. If you have a better way of describing it, then I want to know."

"How about ouch?"

"So passé."

He snorted. "So you just say it for...what? Fun?"

"Fun? What do you mean, fun?"

"It just seems out of place. Your last name is Muñoz, you're from Arizona, and you're Latina...all of those things don't exactly point to—"

"Point to what?" Grace eyed him over her coffee mug.

"Well, Odin, for starters."

"It's called religious freedom, honey. Look it up."

He blinked at her, coffee mug pausing on its trip to his mouth. "You worship Odin?" he asked, looking at her like she might spring a second head or third arm at any moment.

"Well, not in the traditional sense," she replied, hitching a hip against the counter. "But if I did it would be called Asatruar."

"Wait, what?"

She laughed and shook her head. "It's nothing. Stop

looking at me like I'm going to cast a thunderbolt at you. It's just Paganism. Nothing to be scared of, and I don't...follow anything anymore."

"But you used to? I'm not judging, just curious as to the whole Odin thing."

She sipped her coffee, eyes losing their mirth as she thought over the way she had come to use the term, how she had even discovered who Odin was outside of a comic book.

"It's...complicated," she said finally, voice soft.

"Well, it's not like this place has a television, so lay it on me." He slid into a stool at the counter and leaned his chin on his hands as he watched her balk.

She looked around them with raised eyebrows. "No television? What is this? *Survivor*?"

"It's called romance, honey. Look it up."

"Haha, so witty. I like you," She leaned closer and kissed his cheek, one of her hands ruffling his hair as she rounded him to sit at the stool beside him. "You're so much more than a pretty face."

"Yes, yes. Stop trying to change the subject. Get back to the Astral-whatsit."

She stuck her tongue out at him. "Asatruar."

"Yeah, that."

She sucked in a breath and lowered her eyes to the mug in her hands. The steaming coffee comforted her, the warm ceramic in her hands giving her a point to ground herself. It was never easy when she talked about Lilia, which was something there was no way around, not without lying to Anton.

"Have you ever heard of Valkyries?"

"Warrior ladies, right?"

"That's them. Fierce and loyal maidens who welcomed warriors into Valhalla after a battle that pleased Odin, the god they served. I learned about them one day when I was about nine at the library. It was…" She cleared her throat and closed her eyes as she saw Lilia's smiling face in her. "It was a rough time for me and my family because my sister, she—she drowned that summer."

Anton went still beside her. "Grace…" he breathed, eyes wide. "You don't have to tell me about this. I didn't know when I asked."

She opened her eyes and gave him a quick smile. "It's fine. Really. I should, well...it's probably time you found out about Lilia. I mean, she would come up eventually if this continues to be a thing." He nodded, going silent and putting a hand on her shoulder in encouragement, and after a moment she began to speak again.

"Anyways, it was a bad time. Lilia was always so brave and beautiful and I wanted to be just like her. And after she died, everything wasn't right. My family just broke. They fell apart, and it didn't matter how much I did or what I tried, they didn't want to see me for me. They resented me." She sniffled, and Anton made a low sound in his throat before he stood and grabbed a Kleenex from the box on the counter.

"Thanks," she murmured, dabbing at her eyes and wishing she could tell the story without tearing up. "One day that summer, it was only a month or so after Lilia's death, and my mother was in a full breakdown. Now I understand, but then... I didn't. I was scared too, and all I wanted was my mommy. I wanted them to tell me it would be okay, but they couldn't, so somehow or another I got dropped off at the library for one of those lame reading circles for kids. And I wandered off because screw the man, right? They aren't going to tell me to read about Little Bo Peep when I know there's more salacious stuff out there."

He chuckled but said nothing, one hand rubbing her back as she took a quick swallow of coffee. "So I snuck away to the most grown up-looking section of the library, which was filled with all of these old dusty books that didn't look like anyone ever checked them out. And that was when I saw it."

"Saw what?"

"This big book of mythology. It was like an A to Z compendium of gods and all the hijinks they got into, with pictures! Full color ones, all hand done with gold and these gorgeous colors. I must have read it cover to cover...or really just one page in particular."

"What page was it?" he asked, seeing the faraway look on her face.

"The one on the Valkyries," she whispered with a tight smile. "I can still see the page in my head. There was a woman in white armor, just floating there with fire and light all around her, and she had a sword in her hand and this look on her face. She looked so strong, so unafraid, and I was so scared, Anton. I wanted to be like her. I would have done anything to be that unbothered by life."

"Oh, Grace…" His hand froze where he had been rubbing her back. "Sweetheart."

"I knew I couldn't be her because I was nine, not insane, so I did the next best thing and found out everything about them. I read every last book I could. The librarians thought it was weird, but they knew about Lilia, so they gave me whatever I asked for, you know? All those books told me a bunch of random crazy things, but they all agreed on one thing. The Valkyries served Odin, which was the start of my sort of Asatru journey. It didn't really go anywhere, but…" She lifted a shoulder. "Some people have their thing. I have Odin. It just stuck."

"I get it," he said. "Well, not in the same sense, but I get the security of it."

"You get the need to call on an ancient Norse god in times of tribulation because you want to be a Valkyrie?"

"I said not in the same way." He made a face. "I don't know what it's like to nearly devote yourself to a pagan god, but I do know what it's like to wrestle with some good old-fashioned family trauma."

"Oh yeah?"

"Mm, remember how I said that I spent those summers with my very religious uncle?"

"The graham cracker master?"

"One and the same. Well, I didn't end up there for good behavior or family bonding. I got shipped off there when my parents got tired of their fuck-up son ruining the family's good name, because there's nothing quite like the isolation of cornfields and churches to keep you out of trouble."

"That sucks." She put a hand on his arm.

"It did, but it is what it is. When I first got dropped off, I had this silly wild daydream that my parents were going to see what they had done. That they would, I don't know, miss me and come to get me in the middle of the night.

My uncle's house was right next to a highway, which meant there were cars passing by at all hours of the night, and sometimes I would just lay there and watch each set of headlights until they passed, and then I would start over. I mean, of course it was never them, but it was something to do while I rotted away in the Midwest. I used to think it was me. Maybe I was too much...sometimes I still think I am."

Her chest squeezed hearing him say aloud the words she had only ever thought.

"It's not that they're bad people, but maybe people who shouldn't have been parents." He rubbed a hand across his jaw and gave a little shrug. "It's just one of those things, but it's a part of me, just like your family is a part of you."

Grace swallowed hard. The image of a young Anton waiting for parents who never came made her eyes well up with tears.

"You didn't deserve that," she told him.

"And neither did you," he replied, turning to meet her eyes.

They were quiet for a very long time, the chalet comforting like a cocoon around them, insulating them from the outside world.

There was no data theft in this place, in this gentle tentative moment that blocked out the worries waiting for Anton in New York, or the work ahead of Grace.

There was only them, and it was enough.

~

THE REST of the afternoon passed by in that same sort of

dreaminess that had descended on them that morning. Everything felt raw, delicate as eggshells, and the pair moved around one another in that way almost-lovers did, hyper-aware and buzzing like live wires.

Grace knew every move Anton made, and from the way his fingertips trailed her elbow or hand she was certain he tracked hers too.

Even now, with a fire crackling away and soft music playing in the background as Grace mixed cookie batter together, she knew he watched her.

A chilly wind blew so hard that the firs outside bowed and rocked, their branches scraping the roof and sides of the chalet. It was a dreary afternoon; clouds had rolled in off the mountains and settled over the house, but Grace didn't notice. How could she, when she was sequestered away from it all with Anton?

A silly grin spread over her face, and she looked up to see him sprawled on the couch in front of the fire, one leg hooked over the couch arm while he read a book.

There was no scene more pleasing than the sight of a beautiful man reading, and she sent out a silent prayer of thanks to whomever was responsible for the chalet's open floor plan, which afforded her such a tantalizing view.

She smirked, seeing that he wasn't looking at the pages in front of him at all—instead, he gazed back at her over the top of the book.

"How's the book?" she called out to him.

"Enthralling." He turned a page to show her as much. "An absolute masterpiece."

She hummed and added a cup of chocolate chips to the batter. "Is that why you're holding it upside down?"

He let out a sigh, eyes darting away to survey the book. "Seems I've been found out." He snapped the book shut and shot her a wink that made her laugh.

"Why don't you just come over here and stop staring at me?"

"I was waiting for an invite," he muttered, tossing the book to the side and rising from the couch with a stretch. "You've been over here teasing me with all the mixing."

"Mixing is teasing?"

"It is when you do it." He nodded at the spoon in her hand and shook his head. "I've never been envious of a spoon before."

She hitched a hip against the counter. "And why are you jealous of it, Mr. Kovalev?" she asked, and ran her tongue along her bottom lip, one hand giving the wooden spoon a little spin before she lifted it from the batter and swiped her tongue along its length. "Mm, that's good." She grinned as she watched his eyes move from her hands to her mouth.

"Because you've had your hands all over it." He stifled a sigh when she continued to nibble at the dough on the spoon. "And now your mouth is...is..."

It was nice to steal the words right from the man who always seemed to have a quip at the ready. "Is what?" she asked.

"Teasing me in the best way." He took a step closer to her until they were only a few inches apart.

She held the spoon out. "Want a taste?"

"God, yes."

She giggled at the strained pitch in his voice, but the laugh caught in her throat when his hand darted forward, catching her wrist. He pulled her hand up and dipped his head to take a bite.

She almost groaned aloud from the heavy-lidded look he gave her. His thumb rubbed across the inside of her wrist, his fingers sliding up the back of her hand and across her knuckles in a way that made her knees weak.

"Delicious," he told her, and she startled.

"What?" She blinked up at him, her hand feeling like it had a mind of its own as her fingers flexed in Anton's grip. The spoon jerked forward, catching him on the lips and chin before it clattered to the floor.

"Oops." He winked at the dazed expression on her face. His fingers danced across the back of her hand and all she could think about was how close he was to her, how warm he felt, what it might be to have his hands on her in a more physical capacity.

All of it was dizzyingly sexy—and then there was the cookie batter smeared on his face. The last thing didn't detract from his pulse-pounding sex appeal—in fact, it added to it.

"You've got…" She circled her face with a finger to highlight the cookie batter on his. "A little something right there."

He licked at the sweet batter and his eyes closed as he hummed in satisfaction. "That's delicious, Grace."

She nodded, even though he couldn't see with his eyes closed. He had succeeded in licking off a portion of the batter, but there was still the smear against his chin which made her lean toward him to lick him.

She was going to taste this man if it killed her.

"What are you—" He blinked when she nuzzled her

lips against his jaw for a moment before she kissed his chin, her tongue darting out to taste the batter.

"Oh," he breathed.

"Oh," she echoed, pushing herself up on her tiptoes and kissing his lips. She stole another kiss before she sagged against the counter. This time it was her turn to give him a questioning look. He reached toward the bowl, a finger scooping up batter, and before she could ask what he was up to he smeared it across his mouth and cheek.

"Oh no." He held his hands out and gave her a wide-eyed look. "I'm a mess."

"Are you?"

"Absolutely. Terrible accident I've had." He feigned a swoon against the counter and gave her a soulful look. "You *have* to help me."

"And what does that entail?"

Though their words were playful and he grinned at her there was no mistaking the tension in the air, the palpable sexual chemistry which had been rising all day. And if she wasn't mistaken, it was about ready for something to give.

There was no way she would survive until the next day without him touching her, and from the look in his dark eyes she knew he felt the same.

"Kisses. Lots of them. Your mouth all over me."

"Like this?" She pressed an innocent kiss to his cheek, her lips just missing the cookie batter he'd smeared there to tempt her.

"Almost," he murmured, slipping an arm around her waist.

"How about now?" She looped an arm around his neck

and pulled him close before she slanted her mouth to his. She kissed him, the sweetness of the batter pairing well with the heat of arousal threatening to overtake her.

When they pulled apart she ran her fingers through his hair, nails scraping at his scalp, and she gave his locks a tug.

"Is that better?"

He nodded, his hands sliding down her sides, and he pushed her back against the counter. "I'd say you've got the right idea. How about we try that again?"

"Okay," she breathed, her heart racing in her chest as he leaned down to kiss her once more. This time there was nothing slow or tender about the kiss, and her heart soared.

He slid his hands down to hook under her thighs and she had little time to prepare herself before he yanked her up and deposited her on the countertop. He pressed close to her as he stood between her legs.

"Anton," she whispered, hooking her legs around his waist and pulling him toward her by his t-shirt.

He chuckled but allowed himself to be tugged forward. "You're sexy as hell," he told her as he peppered her neck with kisses, while his hands slid beneath her sweater. She sighed at the touch of his palms against her flesh. This was what she wanted, had wanted for days now.

"Back atcha," she breathed, eyes closed and head leaning back while his lips grazed her jawline as he tugged up her sweater. It only took the barest hint of a nudge for her hands to shoot up into the sky. She didn't have to be told when to help, not when it came to reducing the amount of clothes between them.

"You too," she said when her sweater came off and got tossed away. "Lose the shirt, Kovalev." She caught the material at his neck and started trying to pull up.

"Let me," he said, voice muffled by the shirt now almost twisted around him. "You're a menace." He shot her a look of consternation but nevertheless he was shirtless in record time. His fingertips dragged lightly up her sides, the gentle touch making her shiver and wiggle closer to his warm body.

Her breath hitched when he smoothed his palms out and pressed them against her back, fingers dancing up her spine until they met the material of her bra. He cupped her face with one hand while the other unclasped her bra with a sure touch that impressed her. Once her breasts were free, he wasted no time in peppering her chest with hungry kisses, his mouth moving to catch the peak of one nipple as he teased the other into bloom, rolling it between his fingers.

"Yes, but I'm your menace," she gasped, hips bucking as she ran her palms over the firm planes of his chest. Everywhere she touched him there was a new muscle and warm, delicious skin begging to be touched.

There was no way he didn't have a gym in his labs in New York. No scientist was cut like this. His muscles looked sculpted, the doing of photoshop devilry.

"What are you staring at?" he asked.

"You," she replied without missing a beat. Her eyes moved up to hold his, and he didn't miss the hunger in her gaze. "You're gorgeous." Her hands smoothed out against his chest and slid down to drag her nails across his abs, a gesture that caused his breath to catch and his eyes to squeeze shut.

"You're one to talk," he husked out.

"What?" she asked, but her words quieted when he surged forward to catch her lips in a kiss. His hands were in her hair, fingers twisting the pink strands as he teased her mouth open with a flick of his tongue. She moaned when he caught her bottom lip between his teeth and gave it a gentle bite that made her arch and pray for more.

"Anton," she whispered when they parted, though it was only for a second because in the span of a breath he kiss her again.

In her lifetime, she had been kissed and she'd done her fair share of kissing. But there was kissing and then there was *kissing*. And this was *kissing*. The type that left someone utterly wrecked and wanting when it was over.

Her legs tightening around his waist and their hands moved together as they mapped out the planes of the other's body, their breath syncing and pushing their bodies closer with each and every gasp and moan.

She was barely aware of him picking her up from the counter and carrying her. She did realize it when her foot hit the banister on their way up the stairs, and she uttered a barely stifled curse that his mouth stole from hers before it was complete. Once they had cleared the stairs it was only a heartbeat later that they tumbled into the bed.

"Let's get these off, hmm?" He nipped at her collarbone before he caught the waistband of her yoga pants and gave them a gentle tug.

"Yes, yes, a thousand times yes." Grace pushed her hips off the bed to aid in his quest to get her naked. Once he tossed her leggings aside, he divested himself of his pants and before long she had a perfect view of him in nothing but a pair of boxers that did nothing to hide the growing outline of his hardening cock.

"Whoa," she breathed, eyes on the bulge pressed against his thigh.

"What?" He scrunched his face up and paused, face close to her thigh where he had been easing her panties down. "Is something wrong?"

"No, not at all." She shook her head with a jerk. "We are so good."

"If you say so," he replied, leaning back down to kiss the top of her thigh while he hooked his fingers into the waist of her underwear and eased it down.

"I do," she moaned. The feel of his warm breath against her skin made her squirm under him, and she sucked in a deep breath as she reminded herself to breathe when she felt his lips ghost against her hip and then again closer to her barely covered clit.

"Anton," she sighed when he pressed his face between her legs. When she felt his mouth against her through her panties she shuddered at the gentle scrape of his teeth before he pulled her underwear down her legs.

"Holy shit." Her eyes widened at the sight of him between her legs, kissing his way closer and closer. Another kiss and the drag of his tongue against her now swollen labia made her gasp arch her hips up to chase after the delicious friction.

"More. I need more," she begged, but there was no reason to beg, not when he was eager to give her what she craved. She could scarcely remember to breathe as he kissed and devoured with a hunger that surprised her. His tongue pumped in and out of her while his hands stroked her with sure touches intended to not only fan her need for him but to satisfy her.

He caught her clit between his lips, causing her to shout at the sudden pressure, before he pressed his tongue flat and laved her clit with the attention and steady rhythm that made her sob in relief, fingers clenching in his hair as she suddenly came apart.

"Anton!" she cried out as she reached the peak of her orgasm, the pleasure exploding out from her core until it reached her toes and fingertips.

Hell, she was sure the orgasm had made it to the ends of her hair. She felt that good.

She shivered as he continued to kiss and lick, his tongue lessening in intensity and pressure as he worked her down through the throes. The effect was delicious as it prolonged her pleasure, and by the end of it she was sure she could feel another orgasm coiling in her belly.

When she was able to control her breathing she let out a laugh. "That was amazing." She pushed herself up on her elbows to look down at him, still between her legs, arms caging her legs as he dropped a lazy kiss to her thigh. The man had a smile on his face that was the very definition of devilish. He pushed himself up, forearms flexing as he moved up her body until they were face-to-face.

"You deserve amazing," he whispered, nose brushing hers, and she swore under her breath.

"What was that?"

"Nothing, you're perfect," Grace said in a rush, her hands reaching up to run through his hair.

He said nothing but the tender look in his eyes sent a shiver through her that had nothing to do with lust. Instead of saying anything, she lifted her head and kissed him. It was a gesture that he responded enthusiastically to, lips and tongue moving against hers as thoroughly as he had devoured her only moments before.

She wrapped her arms around his neck and arched her hips up against his, a sigh escaping her when she felt the firm warmness of his cock against her. She had just sighed in pleasure, hips arching up again when he drew away with a strangled sound in the back of his throat.

Her hands reached out, following him as he nearly leapt off the bed. "What gives?"

"What gives," he replied, pinning her with a look, "is that you're driving me crazy in the best way." He bent over his travel bag, hands scrambling to pull something out before he righted again, a condom in his hand. "We still have to be smart."

"So smart," she agreed, hands reaching for him again the second he hit the bed. He pulled her close, hands tight on her hips, and she only had a split second of warning before he pulled her down on top of him.

"Is this okay?" he asked, a hand cupping her cheek.

"Yes," she rasped out. All it took was a gentle hand at her waist, urging her forward, for her to spring into action.

When a man gave you *the look*, all eyelashes and want, you acted.

She almost forgot to breathe when she settled above him, her thighs on either side of his hips with his hard length pressing up and between her thighs. She bit her lip and rocked back, relishing the half-stifled moan from him at the gesture.

"Grace," he moaned, hands coming to twist in the sheets as she shifted back, her hands eagerly finding him and guiding him to her throbbing core.

"God, yes. Keep going."

She reached for him and relished the feel of his hard cock in her hand as she leaned forward, scooting up until she was able to guide him into her.

This time it was she who moaned. She squeezed her eyes shut as he entered her with exquisite slowness, and with a gasp she sank down, taking him deeper. The delicious stretch of her body around his cock was downright sinful. She leaned forward, hands on his chest as she rode him, her hips settling into a rhythm that soon The only sounds were their gasping breaths and the delicious slap of skin.

"You're beautiful," he gasped, thrusting up to meet her hips as her strokes began to speed up in earnest. "Drives me crazy. This is so good...we're so good..." His hands came up to tangle in her hair as she fell forward, her hands braced on either side of Anton's shoulders.

She forced her eyes to stay open because he looked at her with such open need that she never wanted to forget it. His eyes were feverish, taking in every detail as she moved above him. That look burned into her, pushing her closer to the edge that she had been approaching, and she cried out as she reached the height of her pleasure.

"I'm going to—Anton!" Her body shuddered, her eyes squeezing shut as she gasped.

He pulled her down, fingers tight in her hair as he

crushed her to him, his lips capturing hers in a devouring kiss that swallowed her cries of pleasure. Her fingers dug into his shoulders while he chased his own end, pounding up into her until he came with a barely muffled shout. His arms were like iron around her as he orgasmed.

In the aftermath of sex, she had never been one to stick around, and she suspected Anton was of the same inclination. But this closeness, the fierce way he held her to him as they both trembled, made her heart stop.

Achingly sweet. Tender in its rawness.

She reached for him as passionately as he did her. Their foreheads pressed together and breath puffing lightly against one another, they slid to the side so that they lay facing each other. He nuzzled her cheek and gave her a half-smile.

"Hey," he whispered, reaching up to trail a finger along her cheek.

"Hey," she returned, leaning into his touch. He pressed a gentle kiss to her lips before his mouth brushed her ear.

"Get some rest, Grace."

She opened her mouth to protest, but the soft touch of his hand against her shoulder as he moved to pull the blanket up and around them stilled her. And when he settled behind her, body wrapped around hers, she acquiesced to his request and her eyes drifted closed.

For the first time in a very long time, she felt at home, and it was a feeling entirely the doing of the man in her bed.

CHAPTER SIXTEEN

"I WILL MAKE *you love physics and your life will never be the same."*

—Walter Lewin

GRACE SHIFTED from foot to foot. She stood in line at the coffee shop just around the corner from the labs. She inhaled and sighed.

Nirvana achieved.

All around her were the sounds and smells of a busy morning; the smell of fresh coffee and pastries energized her, although that could also be attributed to her weekend away with Anton.

She smiled, turning to look at him beside her in line. They had come back early that morning in preparation for a new work week. She was optimistic about their chances of discovering the data thief, and he was invested in pursuing an idea that had struck him on their drive into town.

She glanced at him, scribbling in a small notebook with an expression of concentration that told her he was wholly unaware of the world around him. It was a faraway, focused look that she had glimpsed many times on Lou when she was deep in her work.

Besides understanding that the idea which had sprung into Anton's mind was connected with Lou's research, Grace hadn't been able to follow much of it, which was both exciting and disappointing. The idea had come out of her asking if he wanted an everything bagel for breakfast. How that made him excited, or connected to anything science-y, was beyond her, but she was familiar enough with Lou's work patterns to know when to let the geniuses be manic.

If only she could connect the dots to understand exactly what it was...

"Hey there, Grace!" The barista smiling at her jarred Grace from her contemplation, and she stepped forward with a smile.

"Morning, Marie." Grace gave her a wave. "How's it been around here?"

"Busy. I didn't see you this weekend and got worried. Everything alright?"

"Oh, yeah. I forgot to tell you. I went out of town for the weekend with my boyfriend." She jerked a thumb at Anton, who managed to lift his head from the notebook with an absent-minded smile on his face and a nod at the barista, who blew out a whistle under her breath.

"You two are cute." She grinned at Grace and then began reaching for a stack of cups. "Your usual twenty coffees?"

Grace nodded, already counting out her money. "Please, and whatever bagels you have, too."

"You got it." The barista gave her a thumbs-up, and her eyes widened at the tip Grace dropped in the jar. "Gracie, that's too much! You always do that."

"Listen here, you're like my really cool drug dealer, and I have a lab full of addicts. You deserve only the best the universe has to offer. Now, take my money. All of it."

"Bless you," the barista said, and inclined her head as she filled coffees.

"Back atcha," Grace said, giving the barista finger guns.

She turned, looking for Anton, and rolled her eyes at seeing his dark head bent over his notebook as he continued to write. He'd slipped down into a seat at a vacant table and appeared oblivious to all the hustle and bustle around him, a feat in the busy coffee shop. Whatever it was that he worked on had to be good.

"Hey, space cadet." She bumped his shoulder with her own and almost laughed when he startled. He jerked up from table with a yelp.

"I didn't do it," he exclaimed, hands snapping his notebook shut.

"You and Lou are so weird when you go on a bender," she replied, nudging his notebook with a finger. "What are you working on again?"

He ran a hand through his hair with a distracted shrug. "I had an idea as we drove in…"

"You mean because of the bagel?"

He blinked at her. "Bagel?"

"Nevermind. Tell me about the idea."

He tapped a finger on the journal. "I think I can help with Lou's research if I start over with RED's parameters."

"The stolen infrared telescope?"

He nodded as he paged through his notebook with a smile. "RED was focused on seeing gamma waves—the sort of energy you get when solar systems are created."

"Aren't pulsar waves included in that?"

"They are, but RED wasn't looking at it the way Lou needed. You two are trying to find gravity, to look at the way it operates in space where things are more...bendy. I'm pretty sure I can outfit RED specifically for capturing how pulsar waves behave, and then we can look at the nitty gritty of gravity. It would be perfect with the modifications we are already making to Betsy."

"Really?"

He nodded, eyes still fixed on the notebook. "If we stop looking at the creation of star systems and more at what happens when we control it, then we might be onto something."

"What do you mean, control it?"

He looked up from his notebook with too-bright eyes. "I mean, if I took the lenses developed for RED and modded them to not observe but contain, then we could have a stable environment to observe pulsar waves. I'd make them fit together, like a mirrored cage that would contain the black hole. Then, whenever we need energy, we just open it up and take what we need."

"But that—" She shook her head as she turned over his words. What he proposed was part of a growing trend in astrophysics. She'd attended more than one talk with Lou. Harnessing energy was next on Lou's list of items to explore, once she had satisfied her research on pulsar waves. The woman would support Anton's plan. Undoubtedly it was all a part of her supervillian metamorphosis, and Grace didn't want to go there.

Yes, what Anton proposed was doable, and growing ever more so by the day in the science world, but there was a darker side to it all.

You didn't just pull energy from a black hole using the method Anton described—you *focused* the energy. Most of the research she'd heard concentrated on focusing said energy right into a bomb capable of destruction.

She did her best to not slap Anton's journal away from him.

Upon pain of death she had to keep this far away from Lou and her big science brain. Lou had finally found her footing in the science community. She was respected for her work on gravity wave sources, and Grace aimed to keep it that way, which meant Anton and his talk of harnessing a black hole needed to be put on ice. She stared back at him.

This was going to take fortitude.

This was what she'd been training for, while managing the labs and her science horde. A true test of her science-wrangling skills.

"Anton, that isn't safe."

"It would be, if I designed it."

She rubbed her hands together and tried to choose her next words with care. Glancing toward the barista, who stacked her coffee trays with a deft hand, Grace aimed for nonchalant. "Do you have time for something like that? I mean, with regrouping from RED?"

"This is the ultimate regroup. This is bigger than RED, Grace... this is next-level stuff, and I don't know why I didn't think about doing this before. I mean, Lou and I joked, but I just realized that I was using the lenses all wrong. She's going to love this."

"Love that you're talking about controlling a black hole? Oh, I have no doubt. But don't you think making sure RED makes it to the public in its original form is the best play?"

Containing a black hole meant unlimited energy, but it also brought risks in terms of who controlled it and who didn't. Grace didn't trust the people at the top to not abuse the power of a black hole. She repressed a shudder, thinking of the power something like that would give people who already wanted for nothing.

Anton, it appeared, had a different mindset. Where she saw risk, he saw opportunity.

"This is bigger than RED. It would mean unlimited energy. We could just take what we need, when we need it. What's not to love about that?" He turned his earnest gaze on her and she felt her resolve crack. Just because she didn't trust the people with control over a black hole didn't mean she didn't trust Anton.

"I could give it away," he said, making her look back at him in surprise. "We're talking free energy. It could warm countless homes and power cities, Gracie. Think about it. All for free, and it's clean energy."

"You would give it away?" she asked, and the bright smile he gave her melted away her reservations. She should have known Anton wouldn't keep it for himself. That wasn't the man she was falling head over heels for.

"Of course I would. For what other reason would I be talking about this?" He leaned forward and kissed her cheek. "Don't worry. I'm not going to let Lou blow anything up. I promise."

"Are you sure?"

"Even I know better than to do that," he replied, looking back down at his notebook again. "I did clean the labs after her last science escapade."

She laughed and caught one of his hands in hers. "So you did." She blew out a sigh and then squeezed his fingers. "What do you need to make this happen?"

He rubbed a hand across his jaw. "My research on the workings of star formation and black holes has been focused on making sure others can see it. I need more data to really know what I'm getting myself into. I won't be able to design the lenses if I don't get more."

She perked up. "You need data? I have plenty of data."

"You'd give that to me?" he asked, eyes widening in surprise.

"We've got oodles of readings, if that's what you're after. Tons. So much that we're running a clearance sale. Here." She reached into her bag and rooted around until her fingers closed around the familiar edges of her tablet. "Take this and gimme your phone."

"For what?"

"Just gimme." She made grabby hands for the phone until he dropped it into them. She tapped out a quick note and then handed it back to him. "You're welcome," she said with a wink.

"Cocobeanju1ce?" he questioned, looking down at his phone in confusion. "What is this?"

"My password to unlock the data files on there. Username GMunoz." Grace hopped up from the table when she saw that the coffees had reached the appropriate stack level. "Now come on and help me get these to the labs before the science horde goes off the rails."

"Yes, dear."

"ARE YOU SURE?" Anton asked in what Grace's estimation was the millionth time. He gestured toward her tablet with a jerk of his chin. "That's a lot of data, Grace, and—"

"And what? We can share. I'm the lab queen around these parts—all the data is mine to use as I see fit, and I trust you." She leaned up and kissed his cheek. "Take the data. It's fine. But you have to keep Lou's science hands away from making anything that goes boom."

He held up three fingers. "I swear on it."

"You were a boy scout?"

"Nah, but this looks official, right?"

She rolled her eyes. "Get out of here, Kovalev. I've got caffeine to dole out. You've got data to drown in. We'll touch base this afternoon, yeah?"

"Yeah." He nodded and reached forward, catching her around the waist. "You don't know how much this means to me. It would have taken me months to get anywhere near enough data to even start the designs. You're incredible." His lips just brushed against hers in a sweet kiss that made her lean into him with a sigh.

Sweet with Anton was always good. Sweet was something she'd never had near enough of, and she wrapped her arms around him, enjoying how he held her close, arms sure and strong. Like there wasn't a thing he'd let near her that was bad or wrong.

"You don't have to thank me," she told him, kissing his cheek and resting her head against his shoulder. "Just keep Lou away from anything illegal."

He chuckled, hands combing through her hair. "Now you're just ruining my fun."

"Yeah, yeah." She raised herself up on her toes and kissed him once more, this time with more heat, and when she pulled a groan from him she twirled away with a grin. "Get to work, Mr. Kovalev."

He shook his head, a faint flush dusting his cheeks as he sucked in a breath. "You drive me crazy," he told her, snatching up her tablet with a half-smile.

"I know."

"Lucky for you I happen to like that quality in a woman."

She giggled, earning herself another soft-eyed look from him as he stole another kiss on his way out of the lab.

She let out a sigh and sagged against the table beside her as she watched him go. She still stared after him when groggy-eyed scientists began to filter into the lab.

"Hot coffee, come and get it. There's bagels too." She began handing out caffeine and what was sure to be the only natural food most of the scientists would consume before she forced another meal in front of them.

"Do your heart eyes have anything to do with the fact that I just saw Anton leave?" Lou asked, appearing at her side and snagging a bagel.

"Hate to see him go but love to watch him leave."

"I take it the getaway was a success?"

"Oh yeah, very big success. 10/10 would recommend." She winked at Lou, who made a face and took the coffee Grace offered her.

"You know, as much as I wanted you two together, I'm not ready to go there yet, soooo… how about we review some data readings, and once I'm warmed up I'll give it another crack?"

"Aw, you'd do that for me?" Grace held her hands up to her heart and clutched at her shirt.

"It is my right and duty as your best friend."

"I'm touched." She paused and then said, "Or should I say, I *was* touched. That's the way it goes. I was touched this weekend. Copiously."

"I said I need a warm-up, Gracie." Lou smacked her with her bagel, but she smiled as Grace doubled over in laughter and continued to hand out coffees to the gathered science horde like they were auditioning for the role of Oliver Twist.

Once everyone had drink and food in hand, Grace moved to the workstation Lou occupied and was very nearly ready to take her first sip of coffee when all hell broke loose.

Elisha's panicked voice rang through the lab. "Why are the servers empty?"

Lou stilled beside her. "Empty? What are you talking about? I'm on it. It's fine."

Another voice, not Elisha's: "No. No it's not."

Grace and Lou jerked around to face one another. Fear coursed through Grace's veins.

"Every...ah, everything is going to be okay," she said, twisting her hands. Lou yanked her laptop over, fingers flying over the keys as she accessed the server network they stored their data on.

"No, nononononono, how? *How?*" Lou was quiet in her panic. Her voice barely rose above a whisper as she shook her head.

"How what?" Grace darted over to her side to see the empty screen in front of her which was normally full of files. Data sets she hadn't even gotten her hands on yet, because she'd been sick or too busy on her weekend away with Anton. She frowned and wondered what he made of the empty servers.

She hooked an arm around Lou and tugged her close. "Breathe, boss lady. I'm going to get IT on the phone. I'm sure it's fixable. CERN has backups. We are going to be okay."

Lou leaned forward with her head between her knees, moaning. "This is bad, Gracie."

"I know, I know. Fuck," she whispered, still trying to tamp down the fear steadily tightening its hold on her. She toed a trash bin in front of Lou, who looked worse by the second, and punched the number for the IT department.

A few tense seconds passed before someone picked up the call.

"IT, how can I help you?" The voice was calm, steady, and pleasant in that fake way customer service positions demanded, and Grace grabbed onto it with both hands.

Anything to feel normal.

"Hey, hi, hello," she blurted out, words tumbling over

one another in her rush to speak. "My name is Grace Muñoz. I'm the lab manager for Lou Wright, and we've got a defcon situation happening with our servers."

"What's the problem, Ms. Muñoz?"

"They're empty. The servers, I mean."

"Uhh..."

"Like everything that was on them is now gone. Vanished. Poof. *Gone* gone." Grace rubbed a hand across the bridge of her nose and blew out a deep breath. "We need to get it all back, so please, *please* tell me you can help me do that."

There was silence for a moment before the service tech spoke again. "Sure thing. Just get me your ID number to verify your identity, and I can take a look."

Lou moaned, hands clutching at Grace's waist. At the slight tremor that vibrated against Grace's leg she knew her friend was crying. Grace swallowed, hands going to smooth back Lou's hair as she rattled off her ID number.

"Okay, Grace. I'll open your servers and see what's going on."

"Thank you," she bit out, trying not to cry at the sight of Lou looking so small.

"Well...this is...odd," the tech said finally.

"What do you mean odd? Define odd, because I'm looking at zero files, and that's kind of insanely nightmarish, not odd."

"Yeah, it's that too," the tech replied. Grace could hear them clicking around on their end for a beat before they cleared their throat. "Grace, is there anything you want to tell me?"

"What's that supposed to mean?"

"I just—you are calling about the servers being empty, and it's confusing me."

"Why would that be confusing? That's all of our data from our time here, and before, even. That's easily three years of readings and research. I just, I'm sorry." She cleared her throat and worked to keep her steadily rising voice even. "What's confusing about that?"

"Because you were the one who deleted them."

"Excuse me?" The dread that had been gnawing at Grace bloomed until she could feel bile rising in her throat. "I need you to explain to me what you're saying."

"Okay, here goes." The tech sounded nervous but continued on, "At 8:55 am you logged on to the servers and deleted everything. Now it's 9:03 am and you're calling me asking where everything is and—and well, you didn't just delete it, but you exported everything before you did."

"I what?" she whispered, her hand stilling in Lou's hair. "I mean, I couldn't have done that. I was here in the labs. I haven't accessed the server since Friday."

"Well then, someone with the access code did."

"But I never gave—" The words died in her throat.

"You didn't give anyone your code, did you?" the tech asked, but their voice was distant.

Everything was distant to Grace, outside of the roaring in her ears that seemed to be growing louder with every second. She made a noncommittal sound, her phone coming away from her head as she tried to make sense of what he told her.

Someone with her code had done it. Exported all the data and scrubbed the servers clean.

Someone with her code.

For all her bravado, Grace followed rules. She craved them for the order they provided, a necessity given her line of work, and until today she had never given her access code to anyone.

Not even Lou.

And then today of all days, she'd done it.

Given the info to Anton with a smile and a kiss.

She squeezed her eyes shut, trying to force her breath to come, but it was in vain and before long she had to lean against the table to keep herself from falling when her legs felt like they couldn't support her under the realization.

There wasn't a thing she would have refused Anton. She'd handed her best friend's work, their work, over without so much as a flicker of hesitation.

Silly, stupid, girl.

Useless Grace.

Always missing the mark, trusting too easily, loving too deeply, always eager for warmth.

He'd shown her exactly who he was on their first meeting and she hadn't listened. Anton had taken what he wanted, and she hadn't even realized it.

CHAPTER SEVENTEEN

"Above all, don't fear difficult moments. The best comes from them."

—Rita Levi-Montalcini

"What do you mean, you gave him your access code?" Lou's voice shook, but despite it the woman managed to keep her panic under wraps.

Normally, the knowledge that one's life's work has been wiped away would be a cause for a meltdown, or at the very least some crying or threatening. But not when your best friend looked like her heart had just been shattered into a million tiny pieces.

"I'm sorry," Grace whispered, eyes darting to the side and fingers twisting in her sweater. "I don't know what I was thinking and, oh god, what did I do? I was so stupid."

"You weren't stupid." Lou swallowed and then crossed the room in three quick steps. "Hey, it's okay," she murmured, reaching for her friend, who flinched and took a hasty step backward.

"I-I'm sorry." Grace shook her head, arms wrapped around herself. She shied away when Lou's hand touched her elbow, but Lou didn't let her pull away.

"Look at me, Gracie."

"No."

"Gracie." Lou's voice, thick with unshed tears, cracked, and the sound was like a dagger to Grace's heart. Sucking in a deep breath, Grace finally dared to look up and meet her best friend's eyes. Grace had thought to find anger, hurt...betrayal even, at her foolishness. She expected angry words and accusations to fall from Lou's mouth, but nothing came, and the pair stared at one another in silence.

Finally, Grace spoke. "I'm so sorry."

"I know." Lou nodded, fingers tightening on her friend's arm, and she gave her a watery smile. "I know."

"I didn't think he would steal it," Grace whispered, tears slipping down her cheeks.

What they had lost was irreplaceable. Data from their time in Arizona, from those first long grueling nights and days when they didn't have a clue what they were doing and got by on luck and their trust in one another, in their friendship.

And now Grace had gone and put something above that love and trust that had always been rock solid for them. *What had she done?* How could Lou ever stand to look at her again, be her confidant, let alone work with her?

"I'm sure there's an explanation," Lou said. "I know

Anton, and I know you didn't mean for this to happen. Even if it happened all at once."

Grace shook her head. "They have to be linked. It doesn't make sense otherwise. They said I logged on right before, and I had even given him my device. He had them both. The tech said it came from my device."

"That does complicate things." Lou ran a hand through her hair with a sigh. She closed her eyes and leaned back against the counter, looking tired. Suddenly the spirit that normally made Lou seem invincible had vanished. Grace hated it, but what she couldn't stand was that she had played a part in it.

A silence settled in the room as Lou continued to lean against the table, and the words that Grace couldn't seem to get out caught in her throat.

Apologies were not going to cut it. Not when their work was missing and Lou's career hung in the balance. She had gained traction only recently. There would be no way she could recover from losing her research.

"I love him," she whispered, voice cracking.

Lou smiled, eyes still closed. "I know," she said. "I don't blame you."

"I lost your research."

Lou's eyes popped open. "Our research," she corrected.

"Yours, ours, what does it matter when it's gone? What the fuck are we supposed to do now? If I had just accepted his idea of a fling this wouldn't have happened, but noooo, I had to go ahead and fall for him, and now look at the mess we're in. I didn't even think twice about giving him my code and my tablet."

"Anton wouldn't do this to us." Lou held her hands up

in a placating gesture. "I know it looks bad, Gracie but you have to trust him. You know him."

"Do I? I've known him less than a year—8 months really, and he's only been in the country for a few weeks. I went away with him for a weekend—so what? He *could* be a mastermind thief."

"He had RED stolen, too. Why would he steal from us? He's my friend. And I know he loves you too."

Grace flushed and looked down, shaking her head. "You don't know that."

"You're so easy to love. I hate that your family made you doubt that. It makes me angry when I think about it. I want to shrink-ray them into a tiny ant farm."

Grace laughed and wiped at her damp eyes. "Hey, I'm supposed to be comforting you. What the hell? You aren't supposed to be talking about avenging *me*. I'm your assistant and I gave your work awa—"

"You're my best friend first," Lou said, cutting her off. "And I love you and you love me. That's what counts. I don't care about the research. You were the only one who believed in me before it. I care about you. Stop doubting that."

"It's hard," Grace whispered, but she opened her arms to Lou when the woman came forward. They hugged one another and Grace leaned into her friend with a shake of her head. "You know we're fucked, right?"

"Oh yeah, so fucked," Lou said, voice muffled from where it was pressed into Grace's shoulder. "But we'll think of something. We always do."

Grace nodded, her mind already racing for solutions. Maybe they could review the cameras for evidence. There wasn't an inch of the place that wasn't under surveillance. It was a long shot, but Grace held onto it and was about to tell Lou her idea when she heard a shout from the lab. Instantly, both women tensed and pulled apart with wary looks.

"What now?" Grace groaned as Lou rushed toward the door.

"I don't know, but it doesn't sound good," Lou replied, throwing open the door.

"I swear to Odin, if they think they are going to screw around right now, I'll lose it." Grace stomped after her friend with a glare. Her threshold may be high, but she wasn't a saint, and if there was even so much as a whisper of dissent in the labs she was going to blow the place up herself.

Heads would roll.

"Oh hell," Lou blurted out when she saw Anton standing in the middle of the lab with Elisha staring him down.

"I heard her. Just now. You took her code. You did this." Elisha stabbed a finger at Anton, who held up his hands in defense, though by the confused look on his face he didn't have a clue what he defended himself from.

"What are you talking about? Did what?" Anton asked, head whipping back and forth from Lou and Grace to Elisha. A small group of scientists from both teams gathered around the scene.

"Don't play stupid," Elisha spit out, her teeth flashing, "you know exactly what you did."

"The hell I do. Explain it to me and stop talking in riddles." Anton held up a hand, a hand holding her tablet, and Grace's stomach flip-flopped at the sight. "What is going on? Grace?"

She stepped forward on leaden feet and looked around the room. "The research. The servers were wiped this morning."

"And you did it," Elisha burst out, making the scientists around them gasp.

"He wouldn't do that," one of Anton's physicists insisted, earning a scoff form Elisha.

"You would say that. You're with him."

Lou rushed forward, taking Grace with her. "Look. We need to stay calm. There's no evidence that Anton had anything to do with it."

"She said she gave him her code and he has her tablet." Elisha flicked a finger at the tablet in Anton's hand. "Unless he's suddenly developed a love of scratch-and-sniff stickers, that's Grace's."

Grace colored at the words, but true enough, her tablet sported an assortment of fruit- and pastry-themed scratch-and-sniff stickers she had covered the tablet with in a fit of boredom.

"Grace, what's going on?" Anton looked at her, his dark eyes searching hers, and she found herself moving forward until she stood beside him.

"Our servers got wiped. They took everything."

His eyes widened. "Someone stole everything?"

"It's all gone, and they said someone with my code did it."

He winced. "Who did you give it to?"

"You." Elisha waved her arms, and a couple of the

scientists grumbled in agreement with her. "She gave it to you."

It was then that it all began falling apart. A physicist from New York told Elisha to back off, prompting the woman to threaten him. Lou rushed forward, trying to calm everyone, but the arguments spread to everyone around them.

"You came here to steal from us!"

"What are you talking about? We were ripped off first!"

"Maybe that's what you wanted us to think so Lou would bring you here!"

Grace squeezed her eyes shut, trying to focus on Anton alone. "You," she said, opening her eyes to stare back at him. "I only gave my code to you."

"That doesn't make sense. I didn't do this." He reached forward, catching her hands in his. "I would never do that to you."

"The tech said someone logged on with my code when —when you were using my tablet." She gestured at the sticker-covered device in his hand. "They said someone exported it all and then wiped it. I didn't do it, and no one else but you had the code."

"So you think I did this?" Anton whispered, his face falling.

Grace shook her head. She had to raise her voice to be heard over the others. "I don't know what I think."

"You know me. Grace, you know *me*," Anton insisted.

Memories from the past few months and weeks with Anton flashed before her, and Grace wanted to agree that she did know him, but their first encounter burned like a too-bright star in her mind and the words got stuck in her throat. She sucked in a deep breath, trying to shut out the angry voices around them.

"I just...I need a minute."

Elisha appeared at her elbow. "Don't you dare fall for his stupid puppy dog face. He's a thief!"

Grace rubbed her temples. "Elisha, back off."

Lou shooed Elisha back into the throng of scientists looking ready to start a raid. It was understandable that they shared Grace and Lou's frustration, because they had been working right alongside them all those months.

It seemed Grace had been right in her earlier estimation. She was exactly the same: the girl who loved too big and cared too deeply.

The one who followed her heart to the bitter end.

"I believe you," she said, turning to Anton. "I believe you."

Anton let out a relieved sigh. "I swear I had only just logged into the server when the server crashed. I came back to find you when I realized there was no way around it, and that's when I walked into this." His eyes moved back to where Elisha watched him. "Whatever this is."

"Things are just tense," Grace said, taking his hand, "and we'll figure it out."

Anton nodded. "So long as you believe me."

"I do, but I also think I kind of love you, too."

His mouth dropped open. "What?"

Grace shrugged giving him a lopsided smile. "You heard me."

"What the hell is going on here?" Elisha demanded, stepping around Lou, who had been only just holding her back. "You're holding hands and looking awfully cozy with someone you just said had your code."

Lou darted forward, shaking a finger at Elisha. "You shouldn't eavesdrop."

"I wasn't. I was coming to see if you heard anything, and I heard you through the door. It's not my fault CERN makes its doors from paper, okay?"

"Then don't jump to conclusions," Grace added, raising her chin and squeezing Anton's hand. "Anton didn't do it."

"How do you know that?" Elisha asked. The scientists around her murmured and nodded in agreement.

"I just do. He wouldn't do that to us."

"You mean to you," Elisha shot back.

"That too," Grace replied, and then she squared her shoulders when she noticed the looks of shock and incredulity on the science horde's faces. It was out of character and far from Grace's norm to put anything or anyone above them, and anyone with eyes could see they were in disbelief.

"Did he dickmatize you?" Elisha asked.

"No!"

"Yes. Yes, I did."

Her eyes widened and without so much as a glance Grace landed a sharp elbow to Anton's stomach.

"Oof!" He doubled over, clutching his stomach, prompting an exasperated sigh from Grace.

"Listen up, everyone!" Grace stepped past a still hunched-over Anton. She threw her arms up in the air and waited for the disgruntled, very vocal, science horde to quiet. "Do I have your attention? I love you all, but I'm only going to say this once, so eyes and ears up here." Her eyes moved over the crowd as one by one they gave her their undivided attention. Appeased, Grace continued on, "Right then. I know it's been a very dramatic morning, but I want you all to know that we will figure this out together."

Elisha spoke up. "So losing our entire body of research is now just dramatic?"

Mindy waved her tablet. "She asked for quiet, not your smarmy commentary."

"Your boss is the one who put us in the situation," she shot back.

"No he didn't, because he didn't do this." Grace jerked a thumb at Anton, who only now stood up to his full height and leaned against Mindy while rubbing his side. "Anton didn't steal our data."

"Then who did?"

"I don't know." Grace shook her head. "But it's someone out there. Not one of us."

"Which means we report this to someone who can actually do something like arrest people, and stop accusing one another," Lou said, crossing her arms and giving her team a stern glare. "Everyone take a break while we get this ball rolling."

Elisha relented with a huff and Grace caught her wrist. "Thank you for being ready to fight for us. I just need you to trust me on this."

Blowing out a sigh, Elisha nodded. "I can do that."

Mindy nodded. "If you need anything from us or the New York team, just say the word and we'll get it to you."

Grace inclined her head to Mindy. "Thanks. I'll go start making calls."

Lou held up her phone. "I've got this. You stay here, Anton and Grace. You two look like you need to talk.

"Thank you." Grace darted forward, catching her friend in a tight hug.

Lou wrapped an arm around her and squeezed her. "Love you."

"Love you too." Grace smiled before Lou turned on her heel, her phone already pressed to her ear. Once Lou had left, Anton sidled up close to her and cleared his throat.

"I think you bruised a rib," he said, rubbing his side.

"You deserved it."

He puckered his lips in a pout for a second before he brightened, a wide smile on his face. "You love me, huh?"

"Definitely," Grace replied. She hadn't meant to blurt it out, but now that the cat was out of the bag there was no use in denying it. "I was riding the high of making big declarations and decisions. It went straight to my head."

"Do you regret saying it?"

"What? No. No, never that." She shook her head. "Don't get me wrong, I'm still wondering how it happened, but no. I'm glad I said it, I just wish it had been under...different circumstances."

"When I catch that thief..." He shook his head with a disgruntled grunt. "Absolute unholy terror will rain down on them."

From his clenched jaw to the determined look in his eyes she could tell he meant it, and her heart skipped a beat. The man was absolutely ready to go to war for them —for her—and she felt her breath catch.

"Thank you," she told him, her eyes shining with unshed tears. He started to speak but did a double take at seeing her sniffle.

"Grace?" He swallowed hard, eyes going wide, and held out his hands. "Are you crying? I don't—if you cry—look, don't cry. We will get the data back. I don't know how, but I'll do it."

She laughed. "Are you that terrified of me crying?"

He didn't hesitate for a second. "Yup."

"You're serious, aren't you?"

"As a heart attack, but listen." He caught her hand and pulled her with him, away from where the rest of the physicists gathered. "About what you said before..."

"About loving you?" She followed behind him and did her best to hide her grin.

He snapped his fingers. "That's the one. About that...." His voice trailed off as he led them into Lou's office and shut the door behind them.

"What about it?" she asked.

He stepped away from her, walking into the middle of the office, and crossed his arms. He cleared his throat and looked up at her. "I love you too."

"Oh, Anton." She stepped forward and wrapped her arms around him in a hug. "Please don't feel pressured to say it back. I mean—back there I kind of just dropped it on you. It's not fair to—"

"Grace. Shh." He pulled back and looked down at her. "I love you. Was head over heels for you before I even saw you. I thought my heart was going to leap right out of my chest when you asked me for a relationship the night of the bonfire."

"You mean the explosion," she corrected.

"Yeah, that too." He smoothed a hand over her hair before tucking a lock behind her ear. "I'm in love with you. You saying it first didn't make me say anything I wasn't ready to say, so get out of your head and accept my damn feelings."

"Consider your feelings accepted," she said, and then added, "You're bossy sometimes, you know?"

"Good. Get used to it. Now kiss me," he retorted, earning him an eye-roll.

She tilted her head back, lips already parting in anticipation when he leaned close and pressed his mouth to hers in a tender kiss. It was the type of kiss that spoke of tomorrows, and promised her all the time in the world to continue to get to know the man she had given her heart to.

CHAPTER EIGHTEEN

"Gravitation is not responsible for people falling love." — Albert Einstein

Grace and Anton were still pressed close, their hands roving over one another as they continued to kiss, when the door burst open. She growled in frustration while he continued to kiss her, undeterred by the new arrival.

Grace swore that she was taking a personal day as soon as things returned to a semblance of normal at the labs.

"Hey, knock it off," Lou cried, hands on her hips.

"Mother's home," he laughed, finally releasing Grace, who was still puffy-cheeked and glaring in Lou's direction.

Lou stood in the doorway, and if she had been wearing pearls, Grace was very certain she would have clutched them in horror.

“This is my office,” she exclaimed with a little stamp of her foot.

“Sharing is caring?” Anton tried, giving her a lazy smile.

“STOP PAWING AT MY BEST FRIEND,” Lou shouted, and then continued on in a quieter voice, “I have news to share.”

Grace and Anton shared a look before their eyes shot back to Lou. “What kind of news?” Grace asked, feeling a thrill of excitement.

There was something hopeful in Lou’s expression that had her willing to bet a good thing had happened.

“We caught the thief!”

Anton gaped. “Already?”

Grace’s mouth dropped open. “Are you serious?”

“Oh yeah, I’m *so* serious, and you’re never going to guess who it was.” Lou gestured for them to follow her back into the labs.

“Spill. Now. Go.” Grace grabbed onto Lou’s arm and gave it a shake.

“It was Jones,” Lou told them, and then jerked her chin towards the door before she turned back into the other room.

“Jones?” Grace scrunched her face in confusion.

“Oh what the fuck. Are you serious?” Anton groaned, following both women through the door. In the other room there was a handcuffed Jones sandwiched between CERN security officers.

“He’s been stealing from us since the beginning. He even admitted to stealing RED,” Lou told them, crossing her arms.

Anton's eyes narrowed as he glared at Jones. "He was with me the whole damn time."

"I knew it," Grace whooped. She looked at Anton, who shook his head in disbelief, and said in a quiet voice, "I told you he guilty-scuttled."

Anton rolled his eyes. "Oh, if we had only followed the crustacean identifiers of guilt, we would have all been saved long ago."

"Basically." Grace shrugged, and then looked back at Lou. "How did this happen? We were gone for all of five minutes."

"Try twenty. You two have been sucking face for a lot longer than you thought," Lou told her with a wave of her hands.

Grace flushed. "Time flies when you're having fun."

"So it seems. Anyway, while you two were off canoodling, Jones over here made a big mistake."

"Which was?" Anton asked, crossing his arms over his chest. His eyes were glued to where security officers led Jones away. He hadn't hired the man, but he had selected him for the trip to Geneva. He had been a part of the team to develop RED, and had been given access to every last part of the project.

No wonder Anton hadn't been able to find the thief. It had been one of his own, a possibility he hadn't seriously entertained when Grace had brought it up to him during her stakeout. He'd been blinded by his belief in his team's loyalty, and they had all paid for it.

Who knew he would come to regret his fledgling ability to trust people?

"He came back for his cell phone," Lou said, earning

her incredulous looks from the couple.

"You can't be serious," Grace said. "His phone got him caught?"

"It would be sad if it wasn't so well deserved. Jones spotted you two this morning in a coffee shop, and overheard you telling Anton to take your access code this morning. He knew Anton would be accessing the server today using your ID, so he waited, tailed Anton, and used a program to clone Grace's IP address to log on with Anton."

"What the hell?" Grace shook her head. "You can do that?"

"You can do anything if you're creative and smart enough, which apparently he was, though I overheard him insisting that Anton had never given him his due. Although, if he got caught like this, then I'm taking your side on him not being anything to write home about."

"He was mediocre at best," Anton muttered, pacing now. "He was dependable and that was good for what we were doing, but I have no idea where he got his Dr. Doom ideas of grandeur."

Lou hummed and gave Jones another sidelong glance. "He might have been mediocre, but he pulled it off just like the IT tech told you. He was out of the server before anyone realized what had happened, and was home free before he came back for his phone. I still don't understand it. I mean, he had our data, he had the payoff from RED...can't he just buy 500 new phones?"

"Maybe that one had some great downloaded music?" Grace said. "Quality dog pics maybe—I mean, that *is* worth being caught for."

"Did he say why?" Anton asked, scrubbing a hand over his face. "I mean, why he stole? I compensate well, even if he felt overlooked. Why?"

"Typical villain speech. You didn't deserve the fame and fortune. Blah blah." Lou shrugged. "You had what he thought should be his. It was convoluted at best. Who cares?"

"Because I trusted him. I backed him up when Grace identified his thieving crab walk. That's why. And you know what? I'm going to go handle this."

"Trust me." Lou wrapped a hand around his arm and stopped him when he made to go after Jones. "You're going to want to punch his throat. He's not worth it. You'll have time to get the story from the lawyers."

Anton's lips pressed into a thin line, but he stopped and nodded. "Okay, you're probably right. I'll just...not punch him."

Lou squeezed his arm. "Good man."

"Even though I really, really, really want to, and I feel personally attacked at not being able to feed my id."

Grace snorted but turned her attention back to the matter at hand. There was still an empty server to deal with.

"So now what? Do we get the data back?" she asked.

"Yep, security has it. Jones put it on a hard drive. I'm going to go get that and give my statement. Something you two don't have to do, seeing as you're indisposed." She wiggled her eyebrows at them, and Grace groaned. Lou's eyebrows were positively dancing. "Remember you love me enough to get abducted by aliens with me."

"Odin's beard. Okay, yes. But I want it on record just

how lucky you are that it's true with all the eyebrow dancing you have going on right now."

"Don't I know it." Lou gave them both a wave and bounced on her toes. "Okay, I'm going to go get our life's research back, no biggie, be back in a jiffy. You two try and keep your hands off each other. This is a family-friendly workplace."

"That wasn't in writing when you invited me," Anton called after her when Lou made a beeline for the double doors. "This is censorship!"

"I can't believe it," Grace mused, leaning into Anton's side. She felt gutted, like she had run a marathon, and now that she had reached the end she was simultaneously weak and bursting with energy. She sucked in a deep breath, trying to clear her head of the thoughts racing through her mind.

What now?

How long would it take to get the data back?

When could she resume work in the labs?

And what would CERN have to say about the matter of all the dramatics surrounding their research?

To say the least, Grace was overwhelmed by the list of things that needed doing, but Anton's gentle touch at her arm stilled her. She looked up at him when he put his other hand on her shoulder.

"Believe what?" he asked.

"That we got it back. That it just...worked out."

"Sometimes things work out, Grace," Anton said gently. "And today was one of those days."

"Everything did work out today," she conceded. "It's

making me anxious. I keep expecting the other shoe to drop."

"No, none of that." He tilted her chin up to look at him. "Things worked out today, but even when they don't, that doesn't mean they won't. If things aren't okay, then it isn't the end. And I'm going to be right here for it."

She blinked. Her anxiety was a product of her childhood, of a life lived in the shadows of her grief at losing Lilia. It wouldn't be easy to unlearn the fear, the anxiety, whispering to her that everything and everyone had a timer ticking down over their head, but she would manage it, because like Anton said, if it wasn't okay, then it wasn't the end.

And this wasn't the end. Not by a long shot.

It was only the beginning, and with Anton beside her, loving her and learning with her, Grace was excited for the journey—explosions, unruly scientists, and possible alien encounters and all. With that in mind, she reached out and caught his hand and brought it close to her mouth, pressing a kiss against his knuckles, fingers brushing against the inside of his wrist.

His eyes widened and his mouth parted in a surprised sigh. "I get the whole appeal over hand-kissing now. It's hot."

She grinned up at him and dropped another kiss on his skin. "I love you, Kovalev."

Anton paused, eyes widening before they went soft. He raised Grace's hand to his lips dropping a gentle kiss on her palm. It felt like a promise, but even more than that, it made her feel seen and, above all else, loved.

"You're home now, Grace."

THANK YOU!

Love and Gravity has been a passion project from the start and seeing it in people's hands is a big damn deal. Grace, Anton, and my beloved science horde have a special place in my heart, a place that means even more now that you get to share in that.

Thank you for being a part of that.

You're the best. <3

Sign up for my newsletter e-mail list at https://bit.ly/2PCKCZ1 and *don't be shy about reaching out through social media! I pretty much live for that stuff.*

Reviews help eager readers find new authors to love and we welcome all reviews, both positive and constructive. Drop us a shout and we'll love y'all to the moon and back!

ABOUT THE AUTHOR

Rebel Carter *loves* love. So much in fact that she decided to write the love stories she desperately wanted to read. A book by Rebel means diverse characters, sexy banter, a real big helping of steamy scenes, and, of course, a whole lotta heart.

Rebel lives in Colorado, makes a mean espresso, and is hell-bent on filling your bookcase with as many romance stories as humanly possible!

facebook.com/rebelwrites
twitter.com/rebelwrites_
instagram.com/rebelwrites
goodreads.com/rebel_carter

ALSO BY REBEL CARTER

Heart and Hand: Interracial Mail Order Bride Romance

New Girl in Town: Older Woman Younger Man Romance

Auld Lang Syne: Highlands Holiday

ABOUT VIOLET GAZE PRESS

At Violet Gaze Press we are committed to bringing you exciting new voices in romance, with authors writing diverse, fierce heroines and the swoon worthy men who love them.

If you want to be one of the first to get exclusive content like cover reveals, chapter teases and author acquisitions sign up to our newsletter at www.violetgazepress.com.

facebook.com/violetgazepress

twitter.com/violetgazepress

instagram.com/violetgazepress

Printed by Amazon Italia Logistica S.r.l.
Torrazza Piemonte (TO), Italy

16699856R00164